HEARING GOD

Learning to Identify God's Voice

by Pastor Kent Groethe

Bible Alive Ministries
Fergus Falls, Minnesota

©Kent Groethe, 2005

Bible Alive Ministries
Fergus Falls, MN 56538

All rights reserved. No part of this book may be reproduced in any form without written permission from Bible Alive Ministries.

All Scripture quotations, unless otherwise indicated, are taken from the Holy Bible, New International Version®. NIV®.
Copyrights © 1973, 1978, 1984 by International Bible Society.
Used by permission of Zondervan Publishing House. All rights reserved.

ISBN 0-9768365-4-8 90000

Edit/Format by Joy Minion
www.joyminion.net

Printed in the United States of America by On-Demand Graphics Inc.
Fergus Falls, MN 56537

This book is dedicated to my wife and best friend, Kay. It is through her unconditional love for me in spite of my unworthiness where I have most clearly heard God tell me that He loves me.

Table of Contents

Introduction 6

1. What is God Saying? 12

2. Safeguards to Listening for God 19

Creation Communications

3. Nature 23

4. Conscience 27

5. Gifts and Passions 30

Word Communications

6. Jesus, the Living Word 35

7. The Spoken Word 38

8. The Bible, the Written Word 42

Personal Communications

9. The Senses 49

10. The Mind 53

11. Intuition 60

12. Dreams 73

Supernatural Communications

13. Miracles 88

14. Angels 93

Circumstantial Communications

15. Coincidence 97

16. Object Lessons 109

17. Answered and Unanswered Prayer. 116

Miscellaneous Communications

18. Others 124

19. Fleeces 128

20. Suffering 133

21. Getting Started 142

Other Books by Kent Groethe 155

Reorder Information 156

INTRODUCTION

God is talking to us constantly. We hear very few of these words, however, because we are spiritually dead. An often-stated question by atheists and agnostics is, "If God does exist, why doesn't He reveal Himself to us more clearly?" In reality, He is communicating profoundly and endlessly but we have either very little genuine interest in listening, take no time to try, or have not been instructed in how to do it.

The truth of the matter is: "…God does speak—now one way, now another – though man may not perceive it" (Job 33:14). The Scriptures, our authoritative source on matters of faith, are filled with stories of God communicating in a myriad of ways to both believers and non-believers. Dreams, angels, impressions on one's feelings, visions, coincidences, etc. are common place. Why are there not stories about these today? Some theologians and pastors believe that many of the Biblical epiphanies and encounters between God and humans are fabricated by the authors or used in a metaphorical way only. Many others believe they are true, but hold to a theology which claims that once the New Testament was completed, God quit speaking to His people in any way except through the Written Word. Others believe that these special communications from God to humanity ceased with the Apostles.

I used to be uncertain about why we do not hear God speak to us in ways similar to or as often as He did to characters in the Bible. That all changed five years ago when I began a journey toward listening to God that has transformed my faith in profound ways, and that has changed the way I live and do ministry. I came to realize that I did not hear God because I

Introduction

neither listened nor understood the obstacles to my hearing His voice. Since I have started actively listening, some of the obstacles have been slowly removed and my eyes have been opened to a whole new world where God is deeply involved in human affairs and is actively seeking to guide, strengthen, protect, and instruct us at every point. He accomplishes this by using many vehicles to convey His voice.

The room in which I am presently sitting is quiet. My first reaction is to say that there is no communication of any kind taking place. However, I would not be taking into account the millions of words that fill this room via radio waves. They may be silent to my ears, but they are words none the less. If I turned on a radio in the room, I would access many of those words being delivered on area radio stations. A television set hooked up to a satellite dish would access millions of other communications that occupy the space around me. If I had the means to access these words I would know the present weather conditions around the country, learn how to cook some tasty meal, catch up on current affairs, learn a history lesson, and hear untold other words that teach, entertain, and inform. The key is discovering the right means to tuning in (radio, television, satellite dish, etc.).

In the same way, we are being barraged by communications from God every minute, but we are deaf to most or all of it for many reasons. Here are a few of the most common obstacles:

1. UNBELIEF

Unbelief, I believe, is the greatest single obstacle keeping people from hearing God's voice. I do not mean unbelief in the sense of not believing that God exists or that Jesus Christ is risen from the dead. I mean the unbelief of Christians in the very idea that God is speaking to all people in many ways, and that it is possible to hear His voice if we just listen. The main reason why this is true is simply because most Christians are not told that God speaks outside of the Bible or Sunday's sermon. Many pastors are understandably wary of encouraging their members to seek God's voice through subjective means. There are too many stories of people doing ungodly things because they thought God told them to do it. Teaching that only the Scriptures convey God's voice adequately to believers keeps people safe from these bizarre and dangerous possibilities. The bad news is that people are kept from recognizing genuine contact that God is seeking to make with all of His loved ones outside of the written Word.

Believers are often very skeptical of the notion that God is constantly speaking to them. They can also find it hard to believe that God is interested in helping His people in seemingly insignificant and trivial matters. "God must have better things to do than help me find a parking spot at the mall," is the gist of their conclusions. If people do not believe God is speaking to them in a personal way and about concrete matters in their own lives, they will not hear God speak.

2. SINFUL NATURE

Our sinful nature is naturally cold to divine things. In fact, it kills every spiritual impulse. Paul claims that, "The wrath of God is being revealed from heaven against all the godlessness and wickedness of men who suppress the truth by their wickedness" (Romans 1:18). Paul continues, "...since they did not think it worthwhile to retain the knowledge of God, he gave them over to a depraved mind..." (Romans 1:28). Human sin and the separation from God that ensued have dulled the sensitivity of the human spirit to hear God's Spirit. We have lost spiritual discernment and have grown deaf to the Master's voice. Paul writes:

> *Those who live according to the sinful nature have their minds set on what that nature desires...the mind of sinful man is death...the sinful mind is hostile to God. It does not submit to God's law, not can it do so. Those controlled by the sinful nature cannot please God.*
> Romans 8: 5-8

Not only are we spiritually deaf because of our sin, we are blind as well. Paul says, "The god of this age has blinded the minds of unbelievers, so that they cannot see the light of the gospel of the glory of Christ..." (2 Corinthians 4:4). He also quotes the Old Testament in order to explain this hardening of the human's spiritual sense, "...God gave them a spirit of stupor, eyes so that they could not see and ears so that they could not hear..." (Romans 11:8).

Even when Jesus walked the earth as God's most profound means of communication, people did not understand Him or discern God's presence. The disciples repeatedly misunderstood their divine teacher. The religious leaders confidently concluded that He was absolutely not the voice of God. Instead, they judged Him as being under the influence of Satan.

That dullness to the divine voice persists even when we become Christians. It is a most difficult enterprise to discern His communications, similar to trying to hear radio waves without a radio or watch a television that has poor reception. Paul says: "Now we see but a poor reflection as in a mirror; then we shall see face to face. Now I know in part; then I shall know fully..." (1 Corinthians 13:12).

3. WE ARE TOO BUSY

It is impossible to hear God when one's schedule is full. How can anyone expect to hear the Lord if the day is filled with work, activity, and entertainment? Even when most of us are able to enjoy some time of rest from our busyness, we occupy our mind with television or music. There is simply no room for us to hear God's voice. Mary and Joseph found full houses and boarding rooms when it came time for Mary to deliver Jesus, the Word of God (John 1:1). As a result, he was born outside, away from the hearing and the sight of everyone. In the same way, God's Word, which comes to us in various forms, runs into full lives; thus, when those Words are delivered, they are unheard.

4. WE DO NOT LISTEN

Even if our schedules are not over-booked and we deliberately take time for worship and prayer, we rarely simply sit in silence and listen for the divine voice or reflect on how God may be communicating in everyday circumstances. Fewer Christians every year are spending time in the Bible. Fewer still have learned how to sit and listen to God in their prayer time. God speaks through impulses, thoughts, and a still small voice within – a voice that can only be heard if we stop and are quiet before the Lord.

5. WE ARE TOO FULL OF OURSELVES

The more alive we are in our own flesh and controlled by self-centered ambitions, pleasure and full agendas, the less we will want to hear God, let alone be able to do so. God's voice is relentless in its appeal for us to serve Him by caring for others. This call always demands self-sacrifice and a genuine desire to assist others in need more than to advance one's own life. His call will find an unwelcome reception from anyone who has selfish ambitions and who treats anything that competes with his goals as an annoyance. When one is totally focused on advancing his own ambition, he will be stone deaf to God's call to advance *His* kingdom.

The fuller we are of ourselves, the less room we will have for the things of God. Humility is the key to unlocking our inability to hear God's voice. The more we die to ourselves and yield to God, the more the Spirit of Christ rises up within us and the louder His voice becomes.

6. WE HAVE BEEN TRAINED TO BE RATIONAL, NOT INTUITIVE

Our culture has over-emphasized the rational and logical, and has given us skepticism of the irrational, the spiritual, and the intuitive. We have been subtly trained to believe everything that is empirically verifiable and to dismiss all that depends on faith. As a result, we are poorly equipped to listen to God's voice that most often speaks in ways that bypass reason and is only intuitively heard.

We in the West have all but abandoned the notion that knowledge and information can be received by a person outside of reason. Yet, Christians have always held to the idea that the greatest truths in life, those pertaining to the Spirit, can only be communicated intuitively – that is, by revelation. The mind, in fact, can be an obstacle to this whole process if it proudly thinks that everything can be comprehended rationally. Unless we can be open to hearing in other ways than reason, our hearing of God's voice will be extremely limited.

HOW DOES GOD SPEAK?

In this book I will look at sixteen ways in which God speaks to humans. It certainly is not a comprehensive list, but covers most categories of divine communication. These chapters on the means God uses to speak to us will be preceded by a look at what God is saying through His communications (Chapter 1), and some safeguards to protect people from hearing wrongly (Chapter 2). Below are the categories I will address:

- Nature
- Conscience
- Gifts and Passions
- Jesus, the Living Word
- The Spoken Word
- The Bible, the Written Word
- The Senses
- The Mind
- Intuition
- Dreams
- Miracles
- Angels
- Coincidence
- Object Lessons
- Answered and Unanswered Prayer
- Others
- Fleeces
- Suffering

The first three of this list I call ***Creation Communications*** because God's voice is present from the beginning of the creation of something. God's voice is built into the marvelous, ordered universe in such a way that it cries out, "I am here!" I take a closer look at nature (chapter three), conscience (chapter four), and gifts and passions (chapter five).

The next three communications on the list I call ***Word Communications***. The Bible refers to three different things when it uses the word, "word." The Gospel and Epistles of John refer to Jesus Christ as the Word. He is the Living Word (chapter six). The Old Testament prophets spoke, "Thus says the Lord," and the New Testament Apostles spoke about God's kingdom without always quoting Scripture. These are examples of the spoken word. This is operative today whenever anyone accurately shares truths about God and His work among us (chapter seven). Holy Scripture is the infallible Word of God in all matters of life and space. This Word is written down for us in the pages of the Bible (chapter eight).

Chapters nine through twelve are what I call ***Personal Communications*** because they are words from God that come through different parts of our personality. God can speak through our physical bodies: through our senses (chapter 9), through our mind by pictures and words in our thoughts (chapter ten), through our feelings which I will call in this book intuition (chapter eleven), and through our imagination which best manifests itself in dreams (chapter twelve).

Supernatural Communications are the most dramatic experiences of God's voice because there are no other explanations for them. God speaks in powerful ways through miracles (chapter thirteen) and angels (chapter fourteen).

When God speaks through the normal and natural course of everyday circumstances, I call it ***Circumstantial Communications***. Coincidences (chapter fifteen), object lessons (chapter sixteen), and answered and unanswered prayer (chapter seventeen) are ways in which God speaks to us through the common fabric of life.

Finally, there are three ***Miscellaneous Communications*** in which God talks to us. Others (chapter eighteen) are constantly being used by God to do his bidding. Fleeces (chapter nineteen) are perhaps the oddest of all communications from God, and suffering the darkest (chapter twenty).

I will conclude the book (chapter twenty-one) with twelve ways in which you, the reader, can begin to learn to hear God better.

CHAPTER 1:

WHAT IS GOD SAYING?

My experience has been that God communicates to us for four main reasons. These are His favorite themes. First of all, He longs to tell us that He loves us. He wants us to comprehend how valuable we are to Him. Secondly, He wants to communicate the greatness of His power, His ability and His desire to take care of us. He wants us to have peace in knowing that He is in control. Thirdly, He wishes to guide us in our personal lives. He wants to help us make wise decisions and steer us in directions that will be best for us. Fourthly, He seeks to help direct our service to others so that we can be more effective. He knows the people who can benefit most from what we have to offer.

1. GOD WANTS TO COMMUNICATE HIS LOVE FOR US

God enjoys nothing more than to communicate His love for us. He is like a man in love who is overwhelmed all day long with thoughts of how to express his love to the one upon whom he dotes. Simply put, God is mad about us. He wants us to know that we are constantly on His mind. He wants desperately to hold us and to have us hear His whispers of "I love you."

The Scriptures are, more than anything, God's love letter to His beloved. My wife and I still have many of our love letters that we exchanged as we impatiently anticipated our wedding day, separated by five hundred miles. Our correspondence was full of expressions of longing to be together. God's love for us is even more profound, and He wants so desperately for us to comprehend it.

Paul's prayer for the Ephesians was, "...that you, being rooted and established in love, may have power, together with all the saints, to grasp how wide and long and high and deep is the love of Christ, and to know this love that surpasses knowledge – that you may be filled to the measure of all the fullness of God" (Ephesians 3:17b-19). Paul knew that even though Christians may know in their head that God loves them, as evidenced most dramatically in the death of Jesus Christ, they still have a difficult time comprehending that love in their hearts. This incomprehensible love needs to be revealed through the power of the Holy Spirit. Consequently, God seeks to communicate His love in word and deed, verbally and experientially, to every person.

The Scriptures are a good starting place. We read His letter of love for us and hear His wooing. He declares, "...you are precious and honored in my sight, and... I love you" (Is. 43:4). This love is echoed throughout the Bible. But this divine courtship is similar to human courtship in that words are not enough to adequately convince the other of the depth of the wooer's affections. Actions speak louder than words. I have encountered many Christians who comprehended very little of God's love, even though they knew the juiciest Scriptural passages that conveyed it. However, they came to understand its reality when they saw God provide for them at a difficult time, or when He gave them gifts that could only be traced to His hand.

I grew up with a very poor self-image and carried it into adulthood. As a pastor, I knew well the Biblical statements that declare God's absolute love for all, including myself. I often told others of God's unconditional love for them. The problem was that reading the verses and speaking those true words did not sink in deeply. Subconsciously I could not believe that God really loved me as I was. I did not love myself. Why would God? Consequently, I tried as hard as I could to be good and earn God's affection. The more I tried, the more I became aware of my unworthiness.

To get through to me, God used two individuals who conveyed the Lord's love through their own representation of that unconditional acceptance. The first was Mike Clair, a mature Christian who befriended me in college. He discerned my lack of peace with God, and he convinced me that I had somehow missed the good news of Jesus Christ, that He has done all to make me righteous before God. Mike's words, coupled with his unconditional love, enabled me to comprehend God's love. The second person who helped me understand the love of God has been my wife. More than anyone, she knows me. She knows my weaknesses, my sins, my failures, and the ways I have hurt her. Yet, she has always forgiven me and loved me anyway. I understand God's disposition concerning me better because I see it reflected in her.

The second way in which God has communicated His great love for me has been through generous provision and thoughtful acts that were clearly His workings. One event stands out. A few years ago the congregation I was serving had a three-day renewal event. For one of the activities of this event, we were to spend an hour in prayer each morning for three days in a row. I invited members to meet me at church to pray for our congregation's ministry.

Five people showed up the first day and we met in the basement. The next day, the heat was not working in the lower level, so we met in the sanctuary. There were four of us. During this period I was suffering from exhaustion and, as a result, some depression. I was so tired and unhappy on the third morning that I dreaded going to the church for the prayer time. I did not want to pray, did not want to be with people. I got into the car and immediately had a sense that I was going to be the only one at the church that morning. It was a gut feeling that I knew was God. I also had a sense that the reason for it was that God wanted to spend time alone with me.

Because it is easy to doubt that a feeling is from God, I prepared the sanctuary for anyone who might come for prayer. I kept the lights off and turned on the two electric candelabras that sat on the white tablecloth. Then I retreated to my office, hoping my intuition was right. When nobody had arrived fifteen minutes after the scheduled time of prayer, I knew that I would be alone. I was relieved.

A call from God to go into the sanctuary and meet with Him reached a crescendo I could not resist. It was as if He was waiting for me and whispering for me to join Him. I knew He wanted to talk with me. I finally surrendered. From the office, I entered the sanctuary in the back and headed up the aisle to the altar. As I was walking, I looked toward the chancel and my eyes went to the tablecloth on the altar and the candelabras on either side. The lights were off and the table was set, which created a mood that reminded me of a romantic setting. The only occasion, outside of Christmas, that my wife and I use a beautiful tablecloth, light candles, and turn off the lights are when one of us surprises the other with an intimate meal. I was the last to do it. I had made plans for the kids to be out of the house, put the finest tablecloth on our table, switched off the lights, lit some candles, and prepared a good meal. I wanted to surprise her when she got home. I wanted her to know that I was thinking of her and how precious she was to me. I do this for no other person.

As I walked toward the front of the church, I knew that God wanted me to make this connection. It was a profound moment for me. God had prepared the table for *me*. It was as if He was waiting for me at the altar with an embrace of absolute delight in me as His own. I was deeply touched. I was surprised that He felt that way about me. This experience confirmed the Scriptures that told of God's immense love, and that all I had preached to others to that effect over the years was truer than I had ever dared to imagine.

I approached the communion rail and sat down where people kneel during the sacrament. I simply sat in the warm presence of the Lord and allowed His love to embrace me. I was the apple of His eye, but had not comprehended it personally. I closed my eyes and simply meditated on the awesomeness of His affection. Suddenly, a picture of the woman who had committed adultery and was brought before Jesus in the temple flashed before my mind. It was a still picture of her standing ashamed before the Lord. It was self-explanatory to me. I live with a strong self-condemnation and am sensitive to all the mistakes I make and to the sins I commit. These regrets, and the feelings of guilt that follow, have haunted my life. They have caused me to doubt God's acceptance of me. I am like the woman who had not performed well in life. I was in the temple before Jesus, ashamed and humbled, but the One who knows all my faults and transgressions looked at me in that moment and loved me in spite of myself. As I sat in His presence that September morning, He was saying to my hurting soul, "Neither do I condemn you." I finally understood that He would receive me into His presence, always. When that day had begun, it did not find me at my best. In fact, my performance for Him was poor. My attitude was awful. My heart was cool. And at that low point, He still wanted to be with me. I realized that it was me that had a difficult time accepting me, not God. He was perfectly fine with me. I was welcomed into His presence because of the performance of Jesus Christ, not my own heroics.

God's word spoke clearly of His love for me, but I needed Him to communicate it in many ways before I finally began to understand it. He spoke to me through the love of others. He spoke to me that one morning through intuition, an object lesson, a picture in my mind, and a sense of His presence. He seeks to show His love for all of us in multiple ways. He wants to share that love continually, just as men and women want to express their love daily to their spouses. As we better comprehend this incomprehensible gift, we will "be filled to the measure of all the fullness of God" (Ephesians 3:19).

2. GOD WANTS TO COMMUNICATE HIS POWER TO CARE FOR US

Throughout Scripture, God seeks to reassure His people that He is big enough to take care of them. He wants them to trust Him so that they might not lose heart. Many times, God states to people in times of crisis that they need not fear because He is with them. One beautiful example is found in Isaiah 43. This is His word to the exiled Israelites who despaired in Babylonia:

> ...this is what the Lord says – he who created you, O Jacob, he who formed you, O Israel: "Fear not, for I have redeemed you; I have summoned you by name; you are mine. When you pass through the waters, I will be with you; and when you pass through the rivers, they will not sweep over you. When you walk through the fire, you will not be burned; the flames will not set you ablaze. Do not be afraid, for I am with you...."
>
> Isaiah 43:1-3, 5

We have a God who loves us, but we also have a God who is strong enough to hold us through any crisis. He desperately wants us to comprehend this. If we fail to grasp His ability to guide us and keep us through tribulation, we find ourselves upset, frantic and scared. At times we are tempted to despair. The point God wants to make is that we do not need to fear, although we may still worry and fret. Paul reminded the Philippians of this:

> The Lord is near. Do not be anxious about anything, but in everything, by prayer and petition, with thanksgiving, present your requests to God. And the peace of God, which transcends all understanding, will guard your hearts and your minds in Christ Jesus.
>
> Philippians 4:5b-7

As with comprehending God's love, Paul makes it clear that understanding God's power is something that is beyond natural comprehension. God needs to reveal this great truth through the Holy Spirit, Who uses many means to communicate with us. The Scriptures are full of His attempts to convince people to trust in His care. It is the experiences of seeing God provide and guide through difficult times that convince us of His great power.

I rushed to the hospital a number of years ago when I heard that George Milton, a parishioner, had just had a stroke. It was later in the evening and I was not sure he would be awake. A nurse was exiting as I approached his room. Even though the room was dark, the nurse said that George was still awake. I went to the bedside where I found George on his side facing the far wall.

I did not know how the stroke had affected him and was not even sure he would be able to talk. I told him that I was going to have a quick prayer and then leave him alone. I said I would come back later to talk.

I laid my hands on his leg and prayed. He said nothing. When I saw him two days later he was sitting up in bed beaming. He told me that the day of his stroke, his left leg was the thing that had bothered him the most. He had experienced constant pain all day. He shared that immediately after I began to pray for him that night, the pain in his leg completely disappeared.

God healed George. The problem was that he was not healed totally. He still faced months of recovery and the normal consequences of a stroke. But in that miracle, God communicated to George that He was present and able to care for him. George was awakened like never before to the power of God in his life. He believed that he could trust God. Even where God had chosen not to heal or change the circumstances, George realized that God was big enough to see him through.

Many of the healings I have known about or have witnessed seem to be, more than anything, God communicating that He is strong enough to help. When an individual is graced with a healing, the fact remains that there may have been dozens of times that a healing has not occurred in that same person's life. So why that particular time? I think it is to reveal God's presence and strength, so that in the times when no quick fix is offered by God, we will still trust His working.

3. GOD WANTS TO COMMUNICATE THE BEST ROUTE FOR US TO TAKE IN PARTICULAR SITUATIONS

God wants to help us on our journey. He loves when we ask Him for direction. He knows infinitely more than we do about every situation, and He knows what would be the best route to any destination. In many cases, the Bible may not seem be of much help because it communicates the general desires God has for our behavior, and there is no guidance for particular situations we may encounter in our particular life at a particular time. He communicates in other ways, however. A sense of peace, passion that burns deep within, counsel from a wise Christian friend, a closed door, or a thought that God gives can all reveal the best path to take.

Abraham asked God for guidance when his wife told him to kick Hagar out of the family. His servant asked for help to find the right woman in Haran for the master's son. Solomon asked for wisdom to be a good king. After the resurrection, the eleven disciples asked God to help them realize which of the two finalists should replace Judas. In each of these cases, God answered their prayers. He revealed clearly to each the best route to take. So many of the poor decisions made in the Old Testament stories were made when followers of God neglected to ask for help. God can help us take different routes from what our own bitterness, anger, self-centeredness or greed may encourage us to take. God can give us a sense of peace in our spirits if our decisions are healthy, or lack of peace when a particular decision would be poor.

4. GOD WANTS TO COMMUNICATE HOW WE CAN MOST EFFECTIVELY LOVE OTHERS

God can guide the Christian into more effective service. He knows better than anyone what each individual needs, the best timing to get that need met and the best way to meet the need. For most of the years I have been a Christian, I have assumed that I am to be busy going about the business of caring for other people. The problem is that I also assumed that I was to simply proceed on my own, giving to people in ways I thought were best. There is nothing wrong with this, but there is a better way. Instead of forcing certain acts of giving, God prefers that we wait, pray and watch for Him to open opportunities for our service.

After the resurrection the disciples were anxious to go out and share the good news about Jesus Christ, and they would have done so immediately. Instead, Jesus tells them before He ascends:

> *...this is what is written: The Christ will suffer and rise from the dead on the third day, and repentance and forgiveness of sins will be preached in his name to all nations, beginning in Jerusalem. You are witnesses of these things. I am going to send you what my Father had promised; but stay in the city until you have been clothed with power from on high.*
>
> Luke 24: 46-49

CHAPTER 2:

SAFEGUARDS

I am not unaware of the dangers of trying to hear God's voice, but I believe the benefits of doing so are worth the risks. However, it is important to list several ways that can help us to avoid the errors most often committed in this endeavor.

1. KNOW THE SCRIPTURES

If we are going to listen for God's voice from extra-Biblical sources, we need to have a good knowledge and understanding of the Scriptures. We should read and study them on a regular basis. When Jesus was tempted three times in the wilderness by Satan, it was Jesus' understanding of the Scriptures that guided Him in rejecting the enemy's voice. He quoted three verses from Deuteronomy to justify His rejection of each alluring invitation.

The Bible will have nothing to say, one way or the other, about most of the promptings of the Holy Spirit in specific situations, but once in a while it will clearly steer one away from a word that is not from the Lord. For example, let's say that I sense a strong urge to bring an apple pie over to an elderly neighbor who is all alone. I take it as a prompting of the Holy Spirit and do so. The Scriptures have nothing to say about this action that would keep me from doing it. It does, however, encourage me to think about the needs of others, be kind and generous, and care for widows, things which are accomplished by my actions. Imagine that when I am visiting with the woman I have a sense that I am supposed to tell her that God does not love her because of sins in her past. If I know anything about the Scriptures, I immediately reject this word as not being from God. According to the Bible, the Lord never bases His affections for us on our sins.

2. BE CLOSELY CONNECTED TO MATURE CHRISTIANS

Another effective safeguard in our listening to God is to be closely connected to other Christians who are mature in their faith. When I have a dream, intuitive impression, or other experience that I am convinced is the voice of God, I usually run it past one or more of my Christian friends whom I trust because of their mature understanding of the faith and their spiritual discernment. Clarity dramatically increases when two or more Christians seek God for wisdom on a particular subject. My wife and I often pray together for wisdom from God about certain matters, or ask for better understanding or confirmation of a communication we believe we have received from the Lord. I often include several people in seeking a correct interpretation of a dream.

Many times I receive impulses from God to do something immediately, such as call someone on the phone or stop by to visit a particular person. In these cases, there is no danger of doing something regrettable or wrong because it is always a natural and good thing to make a caring gesture to another person. But if the communication from God requires a major change, like moving to a different town or switching jobs, these decisions do not need to be made immediately. Therefore, an individual has plenty of time to pray about it and to seek the counsel of other Christians.

Several decades ago, a Christian man I knew from the church I grew up in believed that God was leading him take a public stand on a particular issue. The problem was that the actions he believed he was supposed to take would alter his life in a radical way. His wife made it clear that if he followed through, she would divorce him. In spite of this, the man felt compelled to do what he thought God was telling him to do, no matter what the consequences would be. Six mature Christians from the church, including the pastor, met with the man several times. All of these Christian friends were strongly convinced that the man was mistaken in thinking that God was the One behind the impulses he was experiencing. They firmly and clearly communicated their opinions about this matter. The man went ahead anyway and acted according to his convictions, sure that God was leading him.

Recently, I had lunch with a friend of mine and he shared a painful experience from several years earlier. He was a nominal believer at that time, but had a series of clear communications from God through several different means that directed him to do something significant. He followed through in obedience to God's voice, but in the end he assumed he had failed to accomplish God's will. For years, he had been overwhelmed with profound guilt because he had failed God. As I heard his story, I had an undeniable sense (from God) that he had not failed, but simply misinterpreted the mission God gave to him. He had perfectly completed what he knew God had called him to do but had jumped to his own conclusion about what God's ultimate purpose was in it. I then told him what I thought he was supposed to do to finish his mission. I knew in my spirit that what I said was true and he agreed. Years of guilt vanished and he found a sense of peace and a new direction as to what God wanted him to do. He had suffered greatly because he kept these divine communications to himself. Mature Christians could have guided and supported him from the beginning.

3. BE CAUTIOUS ABOUT HEARING SUBJECTIVE COMMUNICATIONS FROM GOD IF SUFFERING FROM MENTAL ILLNESS OR SERIOUS DEPRESSION

My suggestion is that anyone suffering from mental illness or depression should refrain from acting upon subjective inclinations and impressions, even if he thinks it is from God. God often does speak through a person's feelings (spiritual intuition) and thoughts, but it is very difficult, if not impossible, for people who are experiencing deep mental or emotional instability to know whether a particular impulse comes from God or from themselves. People in this situation should depend upon more objective communications from God (e.g. the Bible, the body of Christ, etc.).

I have suffered from depression for over thirty years. When it is serious, I quit trying to discern God in my feelings and thoughts because both are dulled and untrustworthy. Instead, during those periods I listen exclusively to the Scriptures, to other Christians and to certain coincidences in circumstances that show God's providence.

4. DO NOT ACT ON ANY WORD FROM GOD, UNLESS BY DOING SO NO HARM WILL OCCUR IF THAT WORD HAPPENS NOT TO HAVE BEEN FROM GOD

In this book, I am not advocating responding to any perceived communication from God that seriously alters one's life (e.g. move to China, quit a job without having another one in place, do something that offends another person, etc.). I am not saying that it is impossible for God to call somebody to China or have somebody quit a job on faith. I am merely making it clear to the reader that those decisions are beyond the scope of this book. Serious, life-altering changes that are the result of God's voice, communicated in some fashion to an individual, demand special discernment that are confirmed by other Christians and only after serious prayer. This book addresses simple and ordinary nudges from God's Spirit intended to help us care for people more effectively or to find personal strength, comfort, or reassurance of God's love.

The rule of thumb I suggest is this: act upon directions given by the perceived voice of God only if the worst thing that could happen would be either a temporary embarrassment or a waste of a small amount of time and energy, if it should turn out not to have been a word from God. If we go to visit a particular friend because we felt a nudge by God to do so, nothing is lost if it was actually only our personal inclination. To tell a cashier at Wal-Mart that we think that we are supposed to tell her that God is with her and cares about what she is experiencing can bring nothing worse than short-term embarrassment if it is an emotional hiccup instead of God's leading.

5. LOOK FOR CONFIRMATIONS

I trust a certain impulse as being from God much more if it is confirmed by someone else or in some other manner. For instance, I feel much more comfortable that some message is from God if my wife coincidentally reaches the same conclusion, or if that message is conveyed both through a dream and through an intuitive sense. I am amazed at how often God communicates the same message to multiple people or through multiple means. If you have no confirmation on a word from God, simply ask God, "Is this from You?" or, "If this is from You, give me a confirmation of it."

These are five simple but essential safeguards to keep in mind as we begin to listen for and act upon God's voice. If we follow them, we should be as safe as possible from making mistakes that cause harm to anyone as we learn to hear His voice.

CHAPTER 3:

NATURE

Paul states in Romans 1:19-20:

> *...what may be known about God is plain to them, because God has made it plain to them. For since the creation of the world God's invisible qualities - his eternal power and divine nature—have been clearly seen, being understood from what has been made, so that men are without excuse.*

David says:

> *O Lord, our Lord, how majestic is your name in all the earth! You have set your glory above the heavens...When I consider your heavens, the work of your fingers, the moon and the stars, which you have set in place, what is man that you are mindful of him, the son of man that you care for him?*
> *Psalm 8:1, 3-4*

God speaks clearly through what He has created. For thousands of years, most people intuitively understood that the only creator of such a beautiful and well-ordered universe had to be a rational, Supreme Being. What God says loud and clear through His amazing universe is, "I am here and have created all things." The four conclusions we can draw from that one statement are: the world has a Creator; He is amazing and powerful; humans are accountable to this Creator for what they do to and in His universe; consequently, there is purpose in life.

In the West over the past two hundred years science at first was indifferent to the Christian faith, then became hostile and finally rejected the assumption that there was a Creator. Instead, science promoted the idea that all things happened randomly, by chance. Declarations that claimed God as the Creator were completely scorned by academic authorities and publicly ridiculed in academia. Public opinion was wooed and wowed by this scientific world view, and it was assumed that no reasonable person could possibly claim a Creator anymore. The Church retreated from its bold claim that the order and complexities of the universe proved the existence of God. She still believed that, "In the beginning God created the heavens and the earth" (Gen 1:1), but was embarrassed to say so outside of church.

A predominant belief of the scientific community for decades was that the universe always existed, and consequently a Creator was unnecessary. Things have changed. One major catalyst is the strong evidence for the "Big Bang". An inescapable conclusion from this theory is that there was indeed a beginning to everything that was created. If there was a time when nothing existed, including time and space, the difficult question becomes, "How did everything get here?" It is illogical and absolutely impossible that something could come out of nothing, especially without any reason, unless a powerful, rational Supreme Being created it.

There have also been numerous discoveries in the past 50 years in cosmology and physics that have altered some old and now obsolete scientific theories. What this new knowledge has called into question is the once dogmatic belief that natural selection gave a comprehensive understanding of how all things came about (e.g. by chance and through random events). In fact, it is obvious that instead of randomness, it appears that there is purpose behind the creation of the universe. For this universe to exist in the way it does, many improbable events had to all take place at the same time. Simply put, the likelihood that this universe could exist as it does merely by chance is as improbable as the likelihood of me hiking into a wilderness area, where no human has ever been before, and finding dozens of white rocks, all the same size, arranged in such a way that they perfectly spell "Kent Groethe".

In his book *God: The Evidence*, Patrick Glynn states that he was converted from his atheism to belief in God because of "a series of dramatic new developments in science, medicine, and other fields that have radically transformed the old existence-of-God debate."[1] He goes on to say:

> *Essentially, over the past twenty years, a significant body of evidence has emerged, shattering the foundations of the long-dominant modern secular worldview. These new discoveries, it seems to me, add up to a powerful —indeed, all-but-incontestable—case for what once was considered a completely debatable matter of "faith": the existence of the soul, afterlife, and God.*[2]

Diogenes Allen agrees in his book *Christian Belief in a Post Modern World*:

> *Today there are fundamental developments in philosophy and cosmology that actually point to God. It can no longer be claimed that philosophy and science have established that we live in a self contained universe...Both science and philosophy have been used for several centuries to exclude even the possibility of God. On strictly intellectual grounds, this can no longer be done.*[3]

Glynn adds:

> *Ironically, at the very time I was plumbing the depths of philosophical nihilism, unbeknownst to me and to many other people, science was taking a surprising turn. In 1973, in a lecture to the International Astronomical Union in Poland, the physicist and cosmologist Brandon Carter called attention to something he called "the anthropic principle." The anthropic principle, as Western thinkers are only now beginning to understand, amounted to a refutation of the original premis of the overarching philosophical idea: that of the "random universe.*[4]

Needless to say, the shoe is now on the other foot. Scientists who believe in the randomness and chance of all events, and reject the belief that the universe had a beginning, will be in the minority. The Church, on the other hand, will go on the offensive again, with one difference. This time, as the church unabashedly professes God as the Creator of the universe, she will have science standing beside her.

Now, more than ever, people can hear the eloquent voice of God speak of His existence, power, and purpose through all that He has created. The only reasonable conclusion we can make is that, "In the beginning, God created the heavens and the earth" (Genesis 1:1). And with that statement, we can celebrate that everything, including us, has purpose and meaning.

Notes
[1] Patrick Glynn, *God: The Evidence*. (Rocklin, CA: Forum, 1999), 2.
[2] Patrick Glynn, *God: The Evidence*. (Rocklin, CA: Forum, 1999), 2.
[3] Diogenes Allen, *Christian Belief in a Post Modern World.* (Louisville, KY: Knox Press,
    1989), 4.
[4] Patrick Glynn, *God: The Evidence*. (Rocklin, CA: Forum, 1999), 6-7.

CHAPTER 4:

CONSCIENCE

Conscience does not have its source in human wisdom or in common sense. It is not something that the human race created all on its own. It is the inescapable voice of God that He has placed in each person. Whether this knowledge of right and wrong is built within one's DNA or hides in some other area of the human psyche, its origin is the Creator.

It is such a natural reaction for all people to discern right and wrong that it often seems to be merely a simple and natural process of the human mind. This is not the case. In every culture of every age, communities have compiled moral codes and regulations, whether written or oral, with coincidentally the same basic conclusions regarding right and wrong. It seems to be akin to the instinct of birds: they know when to fly south and where to go. Conscience is the instinctive knowledge of right and wrong that is part and parcel of every human life.

Paul tells the Romans:

> *...when Gentiles, who do not have the law, do by nature things required by the law, they are a law for themselves, though they do not have the law, since they show that the requirements of the law are written on their hearts, their consciences also bearing witness, and their thoughts now accusing, now even defending them.*
>
> Romans 2:14-15

Basic moral laws that govern most societies are not products of human creativity and wisdom. They are visible expressions of an invisible reality that exists independently of human reason which is calling humans to certain behaviors and attitudes. In other words, conscience is the voice of God echoing through the lives of every human being.

It needs to be said that a moral distinction between right and wrong only makes sense if there is a God to whom all humanity is accountable. If there is no God, then there is no such thing as morality as we know it. In a system without God, there is no reasonable argument to say that one behavior is absolutely better or worse than another. In that system, everything would be void of moral meaning or purpose. The problem with that conclusion is that it does not explain why, throughout the centuries, different cultures isolated from one another have come to similar ideas of right and wrong.

Conscience is not a result of natural selection, nor is it a natural inclination in humans to nobility. It is the voice of God planted in each personality in order to provide moral instruction and guidance. Its presence in an otherwise self-centered humanity is a glimpse of God in this world. It is the reminder that we are not free to do anything we please without considering the consequences, but instead are accountable for our actions to the God who made us for His pleasure and purposes.

C.S. Lewis claims:

> *Whenever you find a man who says he does not believe in a real Right and Wrong, you will find the same man going back on this a moment later. He may break his promise to you, but if you try breaking one to him he will be complaining "It's not fair" before you can say Jack Robinson. A nation may say treaties do not matter; but then, next minute, they spoil their case by saying that the particular treaty they want to break was an unfair one. But if treaties do not matter, and if there is no such thing as Right and Wrong – in other words, if there is no Law of Nature – what is the difference between a fair treaty and an unfair one? Have they not let the cat out of the bag and shown that, whatever they say, they really know the Law of Nature just like anyone else? It seems then that we are forced to believe a Right and a Wrong.*[1]

The main character in the classic novel *Crime and Punishment* was convinced that there was no God and consequently there was no right and wrong. Consequently, he could do anything he wanted with a clear conscience. A better way to state it would be to say that he recognized that the conscience was an illusion. At one point in the story he killed an old woman, seemingly wanting to prove his theory. The problem was that he could not escape his conscience. Instead of being able to easily dismiss the illusion of right and wrong with a wave of his hand, he began to be tormented by it. In the end, his crime was discovered; with that discovery came a strange contentment as he came to a sense of repentance and faced appropriate consequences for his wrong behavior.

God speaks clearly through our consciences. He communicates that He has a vision of how humanity in general, and every individual in particular, should behave in relation to others. He says that He has a vision for the universe that includes involvement in choosing the right. He whispers that He is watching out for those who could easily be wronged or hurt.

Notes
[1] C.S. Lewis, *Mere Christianity*. (Nashville: Nelson, 1978), 22.

CHAPTER 5:

GIFTS AND PASSIONS

Another example of God's Word being imbedded in the beginning of the creation of something is the unique communication He has shared with each individual when they are born. God has bestowed on every person certain natural gifts and abilities that are only discovered over time. What He says through this is, "I made you for this," or "I made you for that."

He has also instilled in each personality an inclination to become interested in or passionate about particular pursuits. For instance, God makes some people extremely sensitive to the hurts of others. There is a good chance that these people will be most interested or passionate about jobs in the caring professions; nursing, social work, etc. People who have been created with a more cerebral/intellectual emphasis may naturally be passionate about books, teaching, education, etc.

Many Christian teenagers and college students who struggle to find God's purpose for their lives, especially when choosing a profession. Some seek the Lord for help, waiting to hear something intuitively from God that would give them a hint as to His will. Some are very devoted to God and are open to doing whatever He wants them to do. The problem is that God has already communicated many of these things before they ask. To hear Him, one need only discern what are her greatest gifts and her deepest passions. Discovering those two traits will go a long way in guiding an individual, in a general sense, into her choice of career. This is not to say that God won't give us guidance into the particulars: what college to attend, the specific area within a general field of study to focus on, and whom to work for.

Gifts and Passions

Having said this, I need to state that this is not always a hard and fast rule for discovering what God wants you to do with your life. At times, God calls us outside of our natural giftings and passions to perform special assignments. Think of Jeremiah. He loathed his calling as a prophet. It drove him to despair, but Judah was on the verge of being destroyed. Elijah also hated his job. Moses was called to speak to Pharaoh, even though he was not gifted with eloquence. Paul told the Corinthian church that preaching wasn't his forte, although speaking about Christ in front of others was the main part of his job as an evangelist.

A friend of mine is a pastor who is serving in a church that is not suited to his interests or talents. However, he knows God called him there even if it has not been easy for him. When he arrived, the congregation was divided, and several individuals were trying to control the most important parts of the church's ministry. Fighting and disagreements were rampant. The church had become stagnant in its outreach to the community, and its ministry to members.

This pastor is gifted at conflict resolution, even though it is not his passion. In fact, he hates it. In his years of ministry at that congregation, he has dealt effectively with the people who were causing division and has steered the church in a healthy direction again. The problem is that he is worn out. We both have a clear sense that his work is done there and he is presently looking for a new church. His ministry at that place did not call for the use of his best gifts or passions, but it was a special assignment that God gave him on a short-term basis because there was a crisis.

What I am addressing in this chapter is what I will call one's natural giftings and passions. The first step to hearing God on this matter is to get a good idea of what are our greatest gifts and our most acute passions. We can ask the people we know best what they think. We might be surprised at the gifts they see in us that we can not. There are also helpful written assessments that help identify a person's gifts.

When I felt called to be a pastor I assumed that it was to be as a normal long-term pastor. I loved my work and I felt called to it because it was where my talents and deepest passions were operative. There was an obstacle, however. In my first three calls, I discovered that I became depressed after about eighteen months and lost my energy for ministry. As a result, I stayed at each place only three years, and then moved on to rediscover my joy again. All three congregations confirmed that I was called to pastoral ministry as they watched me serve, but I discovered that I was not a long-term pastor.

Eight years ago, we moved to Fergus Falls, Minnesota, where I began an interim ministry. I now pastor churches that lose a pastor and are in the process of searching for a new one. My average stay is only one year in any given congregation. I have discovered that interim ministry is my calling. I've realized this may be because all of the men in my family, beginning with my grandfather on my father's side, have a strong entrepreneurial spirit. We all love using our creativity to begin new enterprises, but lose interest in maintaining them after they are up and running. I do not have any business interest like the other men in my family, but I have the same dynamic at work when I serve congregations. When I come to a church as interim pastor, I start a new venture where I enjoy the challenge of assessing their needs and gifts and help lead them to greater health before a new pastor arrives. Then I move on to another and different challenge. What a thrill for me! It brings out the best in me.

It took me a while to connect my natural gifts with my passions. I was confused when I did not find joy in using my pastoral gifts, but instead found it when I joined my passions with my gifting. We may find that our greatest giftedness is not something that we are passionate about. We may end up giving ourselves to a career that exploits a secondary gift because it is the one that us fill with the most passion. What about our present career? How did we get there? Are we using our best gifts? Is it something that brings our passion into play? If not, we may not be where God has called us. If we are uncertain, we should pray about it. We can also talk to our pastor and friends for ideas and make a list of our gifts and passions. My guess is that most people are not in their God-ordained vocation because they failed to properly assess their gifts and passions early on. They may have gone into a profession because it was easy to do. It might be because it is a family business, and they were expected to follow in those steps. Many settle for a job or a career outside their greatest gifts and passions simply because it provides more money.

We are not always able to exercise our gifts properly because of certain realities. A woman with incredible gifts for music, especially piano, severely injures her right hand and can never play again. A promising athlete hurts himself and has to give up his sport on a competitive level. A woman loses her spouse, and as a single mom moves her three young kids into a rural setting where her family of origin live in order to find needed emotional and financial support. Her natural calling in life had to do with high technology and long hours. The rural area to which she moved has no opportunities for her to practice her profession. In the above cases, realities of life kept them from their natural calling.

Because of uncontrollable realities, our *natural* calling may be unfulfilled. That is when we move toward a *practical* calling. That is, the pianist should have played her gift, but because of certain realities she may end up giving voice lessons instead. The athlete becomes a coach. The single mom teaches computer skills at the local high school, and because of her knowledge guides the school toward cutting-edge technology which significantly enhances its educational program.

If we simply can not fulfill our natural calling or use our natural gifts and are forced into a practical calling, we should not think that it is a secondary use of our time and energy. God can do anything in and through those things that steal our gifts or passions. In fact, we are often guided to a practical calling by necessity, and end up serving God and helping people much more than we would have in "the perfect career."

John Calvin was one of the great Protestant theologians of all time. His natural gift was an incredible brain and his passion was for teaching the faith. But he lived in 16th century France where religious conflict between Catholics and Protestants brought persecution and hatred. He had fled Catholic France because of the persecution, and he set off to teach theology in another country. On the way, a Christian leader of Geneva found him and told him that he was needed to lead the floundering church in that city. Leading the church in this case also meant leading the government of the city. Calvin knew what he wanted to do, but because of the present crisis, he went to Geneva. Through his ministry there, he eventually influenced millions, and continues to do so today. It is doubtful that he would have been so well-remembered if he had succeeded at securing a job as a theology professor somewhere.

In the movie *It's a Wonderful Life*, George Bailey thinks he has failed in life. All of his passions were put on the back burner, continually delayed because of a series of major crises that kept him in the confining town of Bedford Falls to run the family business, a small savings and loan company. He was embarrassed by this line of work because it was dull and meaningless to him, but when he was given a chance to see the world as it would have been without him, he discovered that his work and his life had a profound impact on many. God used him in a greater way through his practical calling.

I want to repeat, if we encounter no obstacles as we pursue employment that satisfies our natural gifts and passions, we should prayerfully pursue using them in the most optimal way. There are often fewer obstacles than we might think. Many people do not contemplate pursuing their giftedness and passions because of money or financial limitations. People stay in a job that they hate and that uses few of their gifts because of the risks involved with changing jobs. Others are too intimidated to go back to school for necessary training or schooling because of all the energy or money it will cost. Some can not stop that restlessness within though, because their gifts and passions are reminding them that God made them for something else.

We also serve God with our gifts and passions outside of our employment. For some, this work is more satisfying and rewarding than their job, because it more closely fulfills what they know they were made to do. Serving God in our churches and in our communities as a volunteer could possibly be the most significant impact we make in the world for God and others, with the exception of raising our children well.

The biggest dilemmas concerning the use of our off-the-job hours for serving are that our time and energy are extremely limited, and the number of organizations asking for help is overwhelming. In our desire to be of help to our churches and community, we often become involved in tasks that we are asked to perform instead of picking services that match our gifts and passions. Consequently, there often is bad stewardship of gifts in most organizations that use volunteers.

The one question we should ask ourselves is this: are we serving God through church and community in the ways He created us for, or are we serving out of guilt, pressure or simply because we were asked? This is where we need to start in assessing our service.

We should make a list of everything we do on a regular basis (great or small) in our personal ministry (outside of work). Then we can identify the activities we're involved in that don't seem to match up with our passions and gifts, and take action. Be brave. We may have to quit or resign from some things, if we can do so without leaving anyone in the lurch as a result. If we need to complete a commitment, we should do so, but then move on. On the positive side, we can make a list of service possibilities that excite us, things that will make use of what we are best at.

The church is often guilty of asking people to perform specific tasks they are either unqualified for or feel no calling to do. As a result, people are teaching Sunday school who should not be. Others are serving on committees who feel awkward doing so. The list goes on. For the church's part, we need to help identify our member's gifts and passions, and then open up doors for them to serve most effectively. Members need to be honest about what they feel called to do, as well as what not to do. The church needs to teach members how to say "no" to requests that are in conflict to their callings. If our members are serving in areas that do not fit them they will dislike what they do, burn out faster, and waste their best gifts and passions.

God speaks to us through the gifts and passions that He put within us from birth. He also refines those gifts and passions through the experiences of our lives. He wants us to fulfill the destiny for which He has created us and listen to what He has already put within. When we do, God will enter the process and will begin to open doors, enabling us to use our gifts and passions in the best ways for His glory.

CHAPTER 6:

JESUS, THE LIVING WORD

In the beginning was the Word, and the Word was with God, and the Word was God...The Word became flesh and made his dwelling among us.
John 1:1, 14

The *Word* can mean one of three things in the Scriptures. Jesus is called *the Word* in the Gospel of John and in the letters of John. He is the Living Word. The prophets in the Old Testament and the Apostles in the New Testament shared God's Word with others without quoting written Scripture. This is the spoken word which spontaneously comes forth from one who had been inspired by God. Then there is the written Word, the Bible, which is the guide for all who follow Christ.

The greatest of these is the Living Word, Jesus Christ. The written and spoken Word simply point to Him and seek to make Him the center of attention. The Living Word, Jesus, is *the* great and supreme communication of God to humanity. It is the communication of His own person, the concrete expression of His incomprehensible love. Jesus is God incarnate, in the flesh, come to meet us face to face in order to tell us how much He loves us. Even though we are great sinners who have neglected, dishonored and disobeyed Him, He would rather die than not have us in a relationship with Himself.

Hebrews states:

> *In the past God spoke to our forefathers through the prophets at many times and in various ways, but in these last days he has spoken to us by his son... [who] is the radiance of God's glory and the exact representation of his being...*
>
> Hebrews 1:1-3

Jesus is fully man but is truly God as well, "the radiance of God's glory." The brilliance of the sun can be seen by the human eye across millions of miles of space. But we are physically touched by its warmth as we stand before it. The heat radiates out through the great distance and kisses our cheeks. We naturally conclude that it is the sun's warmth that makes our lives possible. The concept of God's love is often "out there" somewhere, a million miles from actual comprehension. But Jesus brings it home when He takes on flesh and blood and warms us with the life-giving love of God. We touch God's love. We taste it as we see that God has appeared in person to prove His affection.

Actions speak louder than words. Recently, I married a young couple in our church. Over the past number of years as they were dating, they said, "I love you" countless times. No doubt, they communicated that their partner was their greatest love, and that each couldn't live without the other. However, doubts always linger; we are all aware of how often words are used without thought and without conviction in our world. What confirmed those two people's utterances, however, was that they both showed up for the wedding. Their standing side by side at the altar said much more than the vows they promised. This was no trite saying over the phone or verbal expression of love given to satisfy the other's need to hear it. This act of committing themselves in marriage, of legally binding their lives together, of publicly stating their faithfulness, was the great revelation of what was really in their hearts. They both meant what they had communicated a thousand times.

As unfair as it seems, we naturally are suspicious of God's communication of love through the written Word and the communication of the community. We are veterans of broken promises, words used only to manipulate, and communication that ends up being lies. We hear that God loves us. We are hopeful that this might be the truth but are hesitant to embrace it, but then we hear that "God so loved the world, that he gave his one and only Son..." (John 3:16). God backed up His talk in taking on flesh and blood and meeting us in person at the altar. He has come as a groom who is fully committed to be and do all that He has promised. He really does dote on us, desires us above all things, and accepts us fully, even though we are imperfect. In His giving up His throne and taking on human flesh in order to be with us, He reaches out for our hand and holds it as we stand ready to communicate our love in a life-long commitment. We of course throw in our "I do" as soon as it is time. We glance over to the One who stares back and are amazed that such a One as this would love someone like us. And then, beyond our wildest hopes, He responds, "I do." We can see His face and look into His eyes because He is one of us. As we do, we know that His response is genuine, that He really means all that He says. Actions speak louder than words. Jesus came in person and accepted ridicule, whippings, and a gruesome death on a cross because it was the only way to win us over. This sacrifice is the proof of God's love for us. We can be absolutely positive now that we are so valuable to Him that He would do anything for us. God does love us. Halleluiah!

God's incarnation in Christ is the Almighty's way of using body language to communicate His love. It is no wonder that Jesus said little as He was tried by the Sanhedrin and stood before Pilate. He had no need for words. His body, stretched out over the wooden beams, anchored by the bloody nails, was a most powerful way of saying "I love you." With that act, we can no longer doubt God's attitude about us. His words, "It is finished" (John 19:30), aptly describe how our doubts of His affections come to an end and evaporate into the tomb with Jesus.

CHAPTER 7:

THE SPOKEN WORD

The Scriptures also refer to God's word as that which people speak when divinely inspired. We will call this the "spoken word." The prophets of the Old Testament spoke words from God as given to them, most of the time, through dreams and visions. In Numbers 12:6, God told Aaron and Miriam, "When a prophet of the Lord is among you, I reveal myself to him in visions, I speak to him in dreams." The prophets rarely quoted the written Scripture when they spoke for God, but gave a fresh and anointed Word that God had commissioned them to give. In the New Testament, the Apostles and other followers of Jesus preached the Gospel in such a way that people responded in faith. The believers "were filled with the Holy Spirit and spoke the word of God boldly" (Acts 4:31). Again, "Those who had been scattered preached the word everywhere they went" (Acts 8:4).

The spoken word, like Scripture, is inspired by God and is meant to move the hearers to conviction, repentance, salvation, comfort or service. The written Word is unique in that the doctrines of the faith are infallibly contained in it. The spoken word has little or no doctrinal emphasis. It is instead a word spoken by a Christian who is seeking to speak a truth and apply it to a particular situation. Preaching is a good example of the spoken word. A pastor or teacher who has a good knowledge of Christian doctrine and of the written Word presents the teachings and truths of the faith to a particular audience who need to hear a message from God that is applicable to them at that time. The pastor does not simply read from the Bible to inspire the gathered believers, but uses his own words and illustrations to state a basic truth to people who need to hear it.

The Spoken Word

The Spirit of God inspires faith through both the written and spoken Word. However, sometimes the truth, when spoken in a timely fashion in a way that the audience can understand, is even more effective in inspiring its hearers because it is hand-crafted and custom-made by the speaker for the people who need to hear that particular truth in that manner. For instance, suppose a man who is desperately looking for some reason not to commit suicide checks into a motel, and plans to spend two days contemplating and journaling his situation before killing himself. In his desperation, he grabs the Gideon Bible from the drawer of the dresser and opens it. He spends an hour reading random passages, but mostly stories of the reign of the kings that speak nothing directly to his situation.

When he is hungry on that first night, he goes to McDonald's to grab something to eat while writing of his desperation in the pages of his journal. A Christian man, the same age, is sitting in the next booth and strikes up a conversation. They talk at length and are surprised to discover that they have much in common; as a result, the desperate young man feels comfortable enough to share some of his problems. The Christian is truly compassionate and encourages the man to keep talking. In the end, the believer shares what God had done for him when he faced deep depression years before. He is able to tell the unbeliever that God loves him and wants to help him in his darkness. They exchange phone numbers. The suicidal man receives enough hope to abort his plans to kill himself, at least for the moment. He and the Christian get together again shortly afterwards and hit it off. A friendship develops and the believer invites the man to his church. The formerly desperate man agrees because he is longing for a relationship with God. Through his involvement with the congregation, he commits his life to Jesus Christ.

In this story, a real person was able to communicate not only the Gospel, but the compassion of Jesus Himself. This theoretical person was able to discern exactly what the unhappy man needed to know about God, and to put it in language he could understand. There are many true stories of people as desperate as the man in this story who encounter Christ and receive hope after opening a Gideon Bible. However, the odds of a person hearing the particular truth about God that he needs to hear at a given time when another person speaks it to him are much greater. Also, many people who are thirsty for a word of hope from God will not open a Bible. They will encounter people, however, some of whom are Christians. These people will not need the entire message of the Bible at that time, but only particular truths that apply to their immediate needs. A believer can sift through all that God has spoken through the Bible and apply the most appropriate parts.

People can also translate the truths of God found in the Bible into language and images that best conform to the audience. Paul visited a great variety of people and cultures in his missionary journeys. It would not have been enough for him to simply quote Scripture (except to the Jews, because they already believed in them and conformed their lives and thoughts around the Torah). Paul, like all good missionaries, amended and changed his message for each culture he met, based on how they would best hear and understand the Gospel.

Paul's sermon to the Athenians is a good example of this:

> *Men of Athens! I see that in every way you are very religious. For as I walked around and looked carefully at your objects of worship, I even found an altar with this inscription: TO AN UNKNOWN GOD. Now what you worship as something unknown I am going to proclaim to you. The God who made the world and everything in it is the Lord of heaven and earth and does not live in temples built by hands. And he is not served by human hands, as if he needed anything, because he himself gives all men life and breath and everything else. ...God did this so that men would seek him and perhaps reach out for him and find him, though he is not far from each of us. 'For in him we live and move and have our being.' As some of your own poets have said, 'We are his offspring.'*
> (Acts 17:22b-25, 27-28)

Paul knew his audience and changed his message to fit their thinking. He did not condemn them, but respectfully and tactfully matched his argument to the needs of his audience. Then he subtly introduced Jesus as the Man who will judge all people at the appointed time. Paul did not quote Scripture because he was speaking to a meeting of Greeks who were educated and philosophically astute, and were unfamiliar with the Hebrew Scriptures. Instead, Paul quotes one of the Athenians' own poets! He dressed up the Gospel in clothing that gave it entrance into their world. As a result, many were eventually led to faith.

Both the written and spoken Word point to the Living Word, Jesus Christ. Their goal is to encourage faith in Him. The written Word is the only source of true doctrine, but the spoken word, administered by Christians and in conformity with the Scriptures, can accomplish the same end: to promote Jesus and faith in Him as the Spirit inspires it. As Christians speak about God to others in a timely and tactful manner, the voice of the Almighty communicates to those who hear, opening them to the love and power of God.

CHAPTER 8:

THE BIBLE, THE WRITTEN WORD

Reading the Bible is the easiest way to hear the voice of God. He has given to His church the written Word through which He communicates most clearly to His people. Christians disagree about the exact way in which God inspired the authors of the books of the Scripture, but all agree that in matters of understanding the faith, it is perfectly reliable and trustworthy. All of our doctrines are confirmed in its pages. All other communications we receive from God outside of the Scriptures need to be judged in its light. We reject anything that denies its teachings or professes new truths that contradict it. The doctrines of the faith are established once and for all in the Bible. Dreams, angels, miracles and all other vehicles that carry the voice of God do not and can not present new or contrary teachings.

The Apostles made sure that their proclamation was firmly anchored in the truths of the Old Testament Scriptures. When Paul preached to the Bereans, they wisely "examined the Scriptures [Old Testament] every day to see if what Paul said was true" (Acts 17:11). The Gospel writers went to great lengths to show that the death and resurrection of Jesus was clearly foretold in the Old Testament. When Peter gave his first recorded sermon at Pentecost he explained the movement of the Spirit that day by quoting Joel and two Psalms. When Stephen was brought before the Sanhedrin on charges of heresy, he answered by giving a history lesson from the Old Testament from Abraham to Solomon. His point was that the Christian faith did not deviate from the Jewish religion, which was based on the Torah and that Jesus perfectly completed it.

Likewise, our doctrine, theology, practice and proclamation need to conform to the Scriptures (Old and New Testaments). Where it does not, we are responsible to correct it. The Bible is the driver's manual for the church which describes the Kingdom of God and how it works. We cannot drive Christ's ministry among us without it. God speaks to us through both the Scriptures and His voice to accomplish many things: 1) establish Christian doctrine; 2) reveal the person of Jesus Christ to the spiritually lost; 3) deepen the faith of believers; 4) instruct Christians how to lead a godly life; and 5) comfort the troubled.

1. SCRIPTURE ESTABLISHES TRUE DOCTRINE

When Satan tempted Jesus in the wilderness, he sought to appeal to the most basic desires and ambitions of humanity. He even appealed to the Scriptures and quoted from Psalm 91 in order to justify Jesus' jumping off the temple. None of these attempts at getting Jesus to fail God succeeded because Jesus knew Scripture. For each of the three temptations, He quoted a verse from Deuteronomy in order to reject the enticements of the enemy.

Scripture is still the norm for judging all doctrines and practices. Satan continues to try to lure believers into unhealthy beliefs and destructive attitudes and actions. He still twists the Scriptures to justify unholy thinking and behaviors. The only sure defense is to know the truths of the faith as presented in the Bible. Because the Bible is read and understood by fewer Christians in America every year, the church is vulnerable to attractive teachings that sound godly and religious but are not Biblical.

2. SCRIPTURE REVEALS THE PERSON OF JESUS CHRIST

The afternoon of the resurrection the risen Lord joins Cleopas and his friend who are walking to the town of Emmaus. The two men did not yet believe that the Lord had risen. As they walked together, Luke says that Cleopas and his friend "…were kept from recognizing [Jesus]" (Luke 24:16). How Jesus revealed Himself was "…beginning with Moses and all the Prophets, he explained to them what was said in all the Scriptures concerning himself" (Luke 24: 27). Later they claimed, "Were not our hearts burning within us while he talked with us on the road and opened the Scriptures to us?" (Luke 24: 32). As Jesus broke the bread for the meal after they had stopped for the day, "…their eyes were opened and they recognized him" (Luke 24:31).

Jesus' method of choice in bringing people into a saving relationship with Himself is His Word. But the Word cannot convert the spiritually dead alone. The Spirit of God inspires faith in Jesus Christ through the Word when it is read or heard. Faith cannot be created nor can the Word be received beneficially by humans on their own because "the god of this age has blinded the minds of unbelievers, so that they cannot see the light of the gospel of the glory of Christ" (2 Corinthians 4: 4).

It is interesting to note the passive voice Luke used to describe the two men on the Emmaus road: "Their eyes were kept from recognizing him." The spiritual blindness they experienced demanded a supernatural remedy which was accomplished only as the Spirit opened up their eyes to Christ through the Word. Their hearts burning within them describes the Spirit's work of warming the heart in preparation for the creation of faith. When faith comes it is wholly a gift of God.

My two brothers, my sister, and I became Christians because of the written Word. We grew up in a strong Christian home but by the time we were teenagers none of us had faith. We understood the basics of Christianity, but had no confidence that they were true, and we had little interest in pursuing faith.

After graduation from high school, my brother Craig set three goals to accomplish during that first year on his own: get to know others better, get to know himself better, and get to know God better (if He existed, that is). To help accomplish the last objective he decided to read the Bible. God was neither alive nor real for Craig. His desire was that he would either bump into the real God (get a revelation) or conclude He did not exist and go on with his life without a concern for a Divine Being.

Craig began by reading Job, and as he read his heart began to burn within him. He was eventually reading the Bible for hours a day, his spirit being compelled by God's Spirit to continue. Within three months he had completed the whole Bible. As he read, his faith in God grew and he became aware of a supernatural presence as he read. One evening the Spirit of God fell upon Craig and he surrendered his life to Jesus Christ. It was God's written Word that opened the door for the Spirit to open Craig's eyes to Christ. Craig's encounter with a Living God eventually led three other siblings, including myself, to Christian faith.

Martin Luther called the Bible the cradle that holds the Christ for us. The shepherds discovered the person of Jesus when they encountered the manger. It was that wooden cradle that led them to the Savior. Today, it is the Scriptures that open the door of our hearts to a revelation of Jesus Christ and to a saving faith. It would be fruitless to memorize the entire Bible and remember every detail of it, if one does not come into contact with the Person of Jesus Christ. That is the first and greatest purpose of God's cradle, the Bible.

3. SCRIPTURE DEEPENS THE FAITH OF BELIEVERS
Isaiah states:

> *As the rain and the snow come down from heaven, and do not return to it without watering the earth and making it bud and flourish, so that it yields seed for the sower and bread for the eater, so is my word that goes out of my mouth: It will not return to me empty, but will accomplish what I desire and achieve the purpose for which I sent it.*
>
> *Isaiah 55: 10-11*

The Holy Spirit encourages and strengthens the faith of the saints through the written Word. This ongoing growth and support are essential for Christians because faith can remain stagnant, diminish and even die without proper nourishment. In his commentary on the third commandment in the Large Catechism, Martin Luther states:

> *Even though you know the Word perfectly and have already mastered everything, you are daily under the dominion of the devil, and he does not rest day or night in seeking to take you unawares and to kindle in your heart unbelief and wicked thoughts...against all the commandments.*
>
> *Therefore you must constantly keep God's Word in our heart, on your lips, and in your ears. For where the heart stands idle and the Word is not heard, the devil breaks in and does his damage before we realize it.*
>
> *On the other hand, when we seriously ponder the Word, hear it, and put it to use, such is its power that it never departs without fruit. It always awakens new understanding, pleasure, and devotion, and it constantly creates clean hearts and minds. For this*

> *word is not idle or dead, yet everyone should be motivated by the realization that through the Word the devil is cast out and put to flight.[1]*

There is a crisis of spiritual stagnation in the church today because few Christians read, study, or meditate upon God's Word deliberately or frequently. As a result, most saints are starving, or at least are grossly malnourished. Consequently, the church's outreach and mission can become shallow and mechanical. This is similar to a tomato plant growing in an untended garden. Weeds, animals, insects and lack of moisture can all keep the plant from bearing healthy fruit, if not destroy it completely.

When Christians read and study the Word, they tend their faith like a gardener tends his garden. Isaiah says in chapter 55 that God's Word falls on the reader/hearer's heart just like rain and snow fall on the earth. As that moisture nourishes plants and causes growth, God's Word, accompanied by God's Spirit, nourishes spiritual life and faith.

4. SCRIPTURE INSTRUCTS CHRISTIANS HOW TO LEAD A GODLY LIFE

A Christian desires above all else to serve God faithfully with his life. The Bible is the best source of information on how to do this. It works like a map, guiding a believer from where she presently is to where she wants to go, making her life pleasing to God. Second Timothy 3: 16-17 states that, "All scripture is God-breathed and is useful for teaching, rebuking, correcting and training in righteousness, so that the man of God may be thoroughly equipped for every good work."

In the Bible we learn what behaviors negatively affect our spiritual life and our witness to unbelievers. We are instructed to avoid sexual immorality, drunkenness, greed, selfish ambition, jealously, self-righteousness, legalism, etc. We are reminded of behaviors and attitudes that harm our Christian walk. The Bible also tells us what we can do to please God (not for salvation, which is already accomplished in Christ) and to serve Him in the world. We are commanded to share the Gospel, give liberally and cheerfully, forgive everyone who hurts us, pray for others, meet with believers on a regular basis, care for the needs of the poor and voiceless, work for social justice, etc. The Bible is our guide that leads us into a healthier spiritual life and greater effectiveness in service. As Psalm 119: 105 states, "Your word is a lamp to my feet and a light for my path."

5. SCRIPTURE COMFORTS THE TROUBLED

Through my years as a pastor, I can attest to the power of Scripture to comfort the troubled. There is a reason why pastors read from the Bible to people experiencing grief, despair, confusion or trouble of any kind. People who have a great respect for Scripture as God's Word become calm and reassured when its promises are remembered.

I became an active Christian at age thirteen because of a supernatural encounter with God. I quit doubting His existence and His desire to have a relationship with me. I did, however, doubt that God loved me in my present imperfect condition. I was troubled because I thought that I had to be good or do good things and avoid bad ones to earn God's favor. This misunderstanding caused deep pain for me. One morning I woke up and lay in bed. I began to pray but soon quit because I assumed that God would not listen to a sinner like me. I was a normal teenager who struggled with a lustful thought-life, was addicted to television, and was too lazy at times to read the Bible. I figured that my success or failure in those areas during a particular week dictated God's disposition toward me. After I quit praying that morning, I began to cry. I felt so unworthy of God's affection. I was sure He didn't hear my voice because I was sinful. I grabbed my Bible and opened it. The first words my eyes saw were Lamentations 3: 22-23: "Because of the Lord's great love we are not consumed, for his compassions never fail. They are new every morning; great is your faithfulness." That Scripture convinced me that God loved and accepted me always, regardless of my ups and downs, successes or failures in living the Christian life. It also gave me great comfort and reassurance in the years ahead. Millions of Christians over the centuries have been likewise comforted through God's promises in the Bible.

God speaks powerfully through his written Word to teach right doctrine, reveal Christ, deepen the faith of believers, guide Christians toward godly living and comfort the troubled. It is the most reliable place to go to hear God speak. In fact, many Christians believe that the Scriptures are the only way God chooses to speak to us today. This, I believe, is an unfortunate mistake, for although it is the last word on the issues of doctrine and the best information on the general will of God for all people, it is severely limited in guiding believers in the particulars of their specific lives. The Bible does not guide an individual to his specific God-ordained calling. It cannot direct one to the best way to share Christ with a particular person or open up doors for that ministry to happen most effectively. It is incapable of giving discernment about the presence of God in specific circumstances.

Why would God speak to people in dreams, visions, angels, and other ways throughout the Old and New Testament to give specific commands and guidance, and then stop after the Apostles died? There is no Biblical support for the argument some make that today God only speaks through the Bible. It is from the Bible itself, and from its countless examples of God communicating in many ways, that I am encouraged to do the same. I write this book in order to help Christians identify those other vehicles that carry God's voice, and to give examples of how He speaks in those ways today.

CHAPTER 9:

THE SENSES

> *"The night before Herod was to bring him to trial, Peter was sleeping between two soldiers, bound with two chains, and sentries stood guard at the entrance. Suddenly an angel of the Lord appeared and a light shone in the cell. He struck Peter on the side and woke him up. 'Quick, get up!' he said, and the chains fell off of Peter's wrists."*
>
> *Acts 12:6-7*

God often breaks into our natural world and communicates to us through our senses. He can cause us to feel, hear, or smell something that is really a spiritual reality and does not come from a natural source. In other words, our noses, our sense of touch and our ears can pick up on the spiritual.

1. TOUCH

The angel "struck" Peter on the side to wake him up so he could lead him out of prison. Peter felt an uncomfortable pressure that, if he had been awake, would still have been invisible.

Several members of congregations I have served have bodily felt the presence of the Lord. In each case, Jesus communicated comfort during a difficult time. One woman lost her husband many years before I became her pastor. She was left a widow at an early age with small children. She of course was devastated. In the midst of her profound grief in the days before the funeral she felt pressure of her shoulder that felt exactly as if a person had laid a sympathetic hand there to comfort her. But nobody was there, at least, no human being. She knew immediately that God was present and was communicating that He was there for her. A strong peace engulfed her and persisted through the funeral and the days and months afterwards.

After I had left a certain parish and had moved to another state, friends of mine who were members of that former church lost one of their twenty-year-old twin sons in a car accident. The pain was overwhelming. At one point the father was sitting down near the casket with the surviving son. Suddenly, he felt someone from behind embrace him warmly. He knew instantly that it was the Lord. He turned to his son and asked him if he felt something. The son answered affirmatively. He had experienced the same thing. God communicated His love and presence at a painful time, and brought strength and peace to the family.

2. HEARING

As recorded in the third chapter in I Samuel, the boy heard a voice call his name as he lay in his bed. He did not realize that it was the Lord, but instead, thought it was the priest Eli whose own bedroom was nearby. Eli himself did not realize that it was God speaking to Samuel until it happened a third time. When he understood what was happening, Eli told the boy to return to bed and the next time it happened to say, "Speak, Lord, for your servant is listening" (I Samuel 3:9). When Samuel did this, the Lord revealed something bad that would happen to Eli and his family.

Last year as I lay in bed one night I clearly heard a phone ring, but I instantly knew that it was not our phone. I assumed it was God getting my attention and I sensed that I was to pray. In the night, a phone call is often a bearer of either bad news or an emergency situation. I began to pray for family members and others, as well as for wisdom as to how to pray. I awoke in the middle of that same evening to go to the bathroom. As I lay down to go back to sleep, I heard a cell phone ring. Again I knew that did not come from the natural world. I began to pray.

Just a few days later as I lay in bed, I heard a clear knock on the door. Again I knew that it was the Lord getting my attention and I got up to pray. I shared this the next day with a friend of mine and he said that his wife had experienced the exact same thing the night before also. They also took it as a call to pray. Later, over the course of several weeks, both of them were awakened numerous times by the sounds of telephone calls or knocking. In each case they prayed.

Another strange occurrence that has happened to me a handful of times is experiencing a feeling on the part of my leg that touches my pants pocket, a vibration that is exactly what I feel when my cell phone is set on vibration mode and it rings when I'm carrying it in my pocket. The first time it happened, I instinctively reached for my pocket to get my phone. It was not there. Each time it has happened, I have prayed. With all these occurrences, I spend some time in silent prayer after asking God to help me know what I should pray about. A couple of times I sensed a strong impulse to pray for one of my kids. Several times I sensed a need to pray for our country. The rest of the times, I simply prayed for many different people and things.

Samuel was awakened in the night and told of dangers that were to come. It is possible that God is trying to do the same today, but we are like Samuel and Eli and do not recognize the source.

3. SMELL

Ten years ago, I decided to take a few months off between congregations to write. As that period of time wore on, I began to wonder if I was called to go back into parish ministry. I loved the parish but also had a desire to teach and do more writing. At one point I was completely confused, not knowing what would be best.

Kay and I prayed for guidance. I went to visit my parents for a couple days while Kay stayed at the house where we were living during this interim. This was at the point of my deepest frustration and anxiety about the future. Kay was then reading a book about people's encounters with angels that was written by a Roman Catholic. The first evening I was gone, she nestled into bed for the night and read some of the book before going to sleep. Knowing my worry, she prayed the hardest she had yet prayed that God would give me guidance.

Kay turned off the light in the bedroom when she was tired, put her book away, and lay down ready for bed. She continued praying for me. At one point she became aware of a strong smell of roses in the room. She sat up in the dark. She knew there were no real flowers in the house and that we had no spray or perfume or anything else that smelled like that. It was a very strong aroma. She was perplexed as she lay down again and drifted off to sleep.

Meanwhile, I was in bed at my parent's house, two hundred and fifty miles away. After sleeping a bit, I woke up. I began to wonder again what I should do. I lay in bed and prayed and after a time I began to sense a strong call back in pastoral ministry. Before I fell asleep again, I knew where I was going.

The next morning, Kay picked up her book on angel experiences and began reading. She soon came upon a couple of stories about people smelling roses when a particular prayer was answered. Later I talked to a Catholic nun who attended a seminar I was presenting and I shared Kay's story. She immediately knew what I was talking about. She said that the smelling of roses after answered prayer has a long tradition.

This was a bizarre experience for us. We were skeptical of it being from the Lord at first because there is no Biblical experience like it, but it has a strong history in parts of the Catholic Church, and we have come to accept that whatever it was, God used it to communicate to us that He was indeed aware of our frustrations and was bringing an answer to our prayers.

God can communicate to us through our senses, especially through hearing, touch, and smell. I imagine that many of His attempts to get our attention in these ways go unrecognized because we have not imagined that He works like this. If we continue to miss His communication in these ways, we will be like Samuel who assumed that there was a natural explanation for what he heard. Like Eli, I would like to encourage the reader to explore the many ways in which God has spoken and continues to speak to you, and to respond, "Speak lord, for your servant is listening."

CHAPTER 10:

THE MIND

God seeks to use our mind at times to speak to us. He does this in two ways: by giving us pictures or by giving us words. The difficulty with hearing Him in this fashion is that it can be hard to distinguish whether the picture or word is His or ours. The same problem exists when God speaks to us through our feelings (intuition). These two means of receiving God's communications are the most subjective of all the ways God speaks. He uses our natural processes to incorporate His voice and it feels just like our thoughts and emotions.

One may ask, "Then how would we ever know when it is God speaking or simply our thinking?" The answer is: it is possible to learn how to distinguish the two, but it takes practice. One rule is that the more the thought we have is clearly something that our mind would not think up, or at least not at that particular time, the more likely it is of God. Remember, I am not talking about listening to thoughts that tell us to do something serious or potentially dangerous or obviously stupid. I do not mean hearing voices that tell us to jump off buildings, or tell somebody something inappropriate, or convey a thought that is against Scripture (e.g. "You are unlovable" or "God can't forgive you for this", etc). I am interested in hearing God's voice for instruction or encouragement in the small events of the every day and in my ministry to others.

A good example of God using words and pictures in the human mind to communicate happened for me a few weeks ago. I met with the four leaders who comprise the executive board of our church council to discuss two very important matters relating to the future of our congregation. After we finished the meeting, I suggested that we pray about the issues on the table that day. Before I began, I said that during the prayer I would ask God to speak to us and give us wisdom on the direction He wanted to lead our church. I told them that after that question, we would simply sit quietly in order to listen. I encouraged them to be aware of any thoughts, pictures or intuitive senses that might be from God.

We prayed and spent a couple minutes in silence, listening. When we finished, I asked the group if they "heard" anything from the Lord. To be honest, I assumed that nothing would come of this. This was all new for these Lutherans and they had never practiced such a thing as this before. I also knew that there would be a fear of saying something, even if they did hear God's voice, because it might not be of God and they would look foolish. Was I ever wrong! Three out of the four were confident that God had told them something.

One woman said that she had a strong feeling (spiritual intuition) that a particular decision we had just made during the meeting was pleasing to God. Two others shared that they believed that God had given them thoughts. One man had a picture/image and a certain woman had words in her mind. The man saw a locked door and nothing else. The woman said that during the prayer she had a particular Bible verse go through her mind repeatedly, "I stand at the door and knock" (Revelation 3: 20). We found it interesting that both thoughts conveyed a shut door. This coincidence seemed to confirm that it was God speaking. When we left that morning, we were not sure what those thoughts from God communicated.

Two days later, I got a call from a woman in our congregation who wanted to share two dreams that she had had in one night recently. She, nor anyone else, knew the contents of the executive board meeting the Sunday before, let alone the two door images. This woman believed that the dreams were from God and that it had to do with our congregation. After hearing them, I agreed. In one of her short dreams, I stood before a locked door with a key to it. There was more that happened in the dreams, and after praying about them and sharing them with two people from the executive board, I began to get an idea of their meanings. All three images together guided us to an interpretation that is changing our church's direction in a particular area. I cannot share it all here because it is still incomplete and may take a couple years to unfold. It had to do with in-house matters of our congregation.

The Mind

PICTURES

My wife hears from God most often through pictures He puts in her mind. This usually happens when we are praying together for wisdom and direction on a particular matter and sit silently before God, listening. While praying recently for a young girl, she saw a picture of a bumpy road and the girl was driving a car over it. It was an uneven ride, but the car made it and kept going. Afterwards, we both sensed that the image talked about some problems that were to come up in this teenage girl's life, but nothing that will keep her from going in the right direction. Kay has had many other images during prayer that have guided us in knowing how to pray for a particular person or matter. I myself have received few pictures in this way.

It is not uncommon for God to put particular people on our minds because He either wants us to visit them or simply to pray for them. These pictures often come at a time when our mind is not thinking about that person, nor would our thoughts have gone to that person unaided. I was leaving a nursing home one morning and as I left the parking lot, out of the blue I thought about a particular pastor who was relatively new in town at the time. It was evident to me that the thought was an intrusion to the natural thoughts with which my mind was engaged at that moment.

I changed directions and went toward the church that the pastor served. When I stopped at the secretary's office, she said that he was presently in a meeting. She was going to leave a written message for him from me but all of a sudden decided to buzz his office and check to see if he could possibly see me. He said yes, and came out to visit with me within a couple of minutes. We were not acquainted with each other, so we visited about personal matters before he gave me a tour of his church. As we walked and finally ended up standing together in the sanctuary, we were engaged in a delightful conversation about ministry and theology. It was a very uplifting connection. Toward the end of our talk, he mentioned that he had been a little discouraged lately with some aspects of the ministry. That morning while having a prayer time with his wife he expressed his frustrations and asked God to send him somebody to give him encouragement that day. He took my timely visit as his answer.

I never would have stopped by to see him if I had not acted on a picture God put in my mind. What a thrill to be used by God in that way to encourage a brother in the Lord. It was another example of how much God cares for His people and is engaged in guiding and providing for them continually. Imagine how much better He could take care of us if we were more in tune with His voice.

About six months ago I was invited to give a short talk for a group of women at a church in a nearby community. They were holding a mini-retreat. I was supposed to begin at 10:00 in the evening. It was winter, so as I left my house at 9:30, it was pitch-black when I went out the door. I could not see anything, so I stumbled blindly the hundred or so feet to the car. Just as I was getting close, I was startled to feel a moving object brush against my hand. After I recovered from my initial shock, I reached out my hand and felt a large dog. We do not have a dog and have only a few neighbors around us in the country, so I was confused about where she had come from. It was so out of place and so striking that I prayed for understanding if it was a word from God.

The Lord used a dog in my life, or the image of a dog, to symbolize "man's best friend" – in other words, Jesus. The dog gently communicated his presence when I was struggling to find my way in the dark. I did not conclude that I personally, at the time, needed a word of comfort that Jesus was present in my darkness and was encouraging me on. I wondered if it was a word from God for the woman's retreat at which I was soon to speak.

At the church, the seven women and I gathered in the sanctuary at a little after ten. We were all clustered together in the first two pews on one side and began with singing a couple hymns.

When it was my time to speak, I said that I wanted to begin with prayer and then have a time of silence in the presence of God. I told them to pay attention to any thoughts or gut-feelings that may be the voice of God. We prayed, sat before the Lord in quiet, and then I asked if anybody sensed God communicating a specific word to us.

I began by saying that I thought that I was supposed to share something that came as an object lesson before I arrived that night (the dog encounter). I said that I believed that God wanted to tell somebody, or more than one person, that He knows that she was going through a dark and difficult time. I went on to say that there might be someone there who had been desperate for a "best friend" from whom to find support and encouragement, but had been unsuccessful. As a result, that person was lonely. "Jesus wants to tell you," I continued, "that He is your best friend." I also said that He is present with her in her time of darkness.

I had a strong sense that the dog object lesson was indeed a word from the Lord for a woman there that night. I sensed that my word was a proper interpretation of that word as well. And yet, who was I to think that I actually had heard God communicate to one or more of these women through me? I decided to take a risk and deliver that message, because the worst thing that could have happened was that I would be embarrassed if I was wrong. I knew that unless I began to act on these possible words from God, I would never know whether He actually did this sort of thing today.

Shortly after sharing, one teary-eyed woman shared that she had been desperately longing for a best friend, but had been unsuccessful in finding one. She shared about several circumstances that had made her life very difficult. She took the object lesson as a word from God for her. I think she basked in the wonder of God's great love for her and His special contact to encourage her. That night she realized that she had *always had* a best friend.

We stopped everything and laid our hands on the woman and prayed. When we had concluded, I shared with everyone that I had seen a picture of a beautiful flower as I prayed for the woman. I said to the woman that I thought that was how God viewed her, as a beautiful part of His creation. From the sounds a couple of the women made, I realized that I had said something relevant. One participant asked me if I had known that this woman was a fanatic when it came to flowers. In that small town she was known as the "Flower Lady." That convinced me that the picture was from God and meant for that woman. God is so great! He must be frustrated that we miss a vast majority of His love notes and thoughtful acts because we do not know how to hear His voice.

I asked the group of women if they had "heard" anything else during our prayer time. One woman said she was given a picture of Jesus standing in the sanctuary in front of and a little to the right of where they were seated. She pointed to the place where she saw that picture in her mind. He was looking at the group, she continued, like a proud father looks at his child. She was moved by this image. Another woman then said that she had also seen a picture of Jesus with a look of deep affection for everyone there and He stood in the same place as the other woman had seen Him. These similar pictures put into two separate minds confirmed to everyone that we were given a picture from God Himself revealing His disposition toward us. We were all moved.

After a couple more women shared, I told them that I discerned that I was not supposed to give my message after all. God had decided to speak Himself. Besides, how could I follow a message like that? I cannot adequately convey to you the awe I felt to be present when God spoke to these women whom He loved. It was much more satisfying than to speak myself and receive praise for it.

God speaks to us by putting pictures in our minds that communicate the right message to us at the right time. It is much like a daydream (vision), except that it is more like a snapshot from a camera, while visions are pictures in one's mind that are like a movie. Both give us valuable insights into the thoughts God has toward us.

WORDS

A second way in which God speaks through our minds is through actual words, or even just one word which is foreign to where our mind was at or to what we would have thought.

My brother Craig was with a friend at a lake cabin our family once owned almost thirty years ago. They were on the lake fishing about half a mile from the house when a sudden storm turned glass-calm waters into four-foot waves in just minutes. Craig was driving the boat, and at one point concluded that the ill-equipped vessel would not stay afloat for long. As you might expect, he was filled with great fear. All of a sudden, these words went through his mind in a clear and strong fashion, "Who are you going to fear, me or the storm." I know it is bad English, but Craig knew it was the Lord because these words were foreign to where his thoughts were at the time. In that moment, Craig knew that he was not alone. "You!" he shouted. Immediately, a deep peace enveloped him, one that no human can experience apart from the Spirit of God. Craig's fear immediately disappeared. He stopped worrying and realized that he was all right, whether the boat made it to shore or capsized. In the end they made it and Craig's friend, shaken by the experience, gave his life to the Lord.

Mike is a great friend and brother in Christ. He is also very sensitive to God's voice and leading. I live in Minnesota and Mike lives in Georgia. Though we love each other dearly, neither of us is good at staying in touch. We have probably connected, on average, two or three times a year in the past decade.

When I was suffering through two-and-a-half years of exhaustion and depression, I told him about it when I made a rare visit to Georgia. He knew that I had quit writing and wondered if I would ever write again. Six months went by without any new contact with him. It was August, and I went to a spiritual life conference for a few days. It was there that God began to heal me and do a work in me. After two-and-a-half desperate years, I returned home from the conference renewed and feeling the best I had in a long, long time. From that week on, I continuously improved until I was well. When I got home, my wife said that Mike had called several times wanting to talk to me. I called him back and he said that he had sensed that something good was going on with my health (I had had no contact with him for the past six months). I told him what had happened to me at the conference and that I thought that my long trek through the dark valley was over.

He told me God had put me on his heart and he had been praying for me several times a day for a week. He sensed that something good was happening to me. During one prayer for me he had the following words

The Mind

pass through his mind, "The pen will not be idle long." That was a great encouragement for me because after three years with no energy or creativity, I could not imagine ever writing again. Soon after this, my joy and energy returned and I returned to writing.

I have heard many Christians talk about how they were comforted or guided by thoughts that they knew were from God. We do not, however, have any concrete examples in Acts of the Apostles or other early Christians hearing from God in this way. It is probably not that it didn't happen, but they did not record it. In the New Testament, there are a number of references to God giving his followers guidance through the Holy Spirit's revelation, but Scripture does not say exactly how that happened. Luke records that "the Holy Spirit was upon him" and "it had been revealed to him by the Holy Spirit that he would not die before he had seen the [Messiah]" (Luke 2: 25b-26). Luke also records that "the Spirit told Philip, 'Go to that chariot and stay near it'" (Acts 8:29). Paul and his traveling companions were "kept by the Holy Spirit from preaching the word in...Asia" (Acts 16:6), and then when they attempted to enter Bithynia, Luke writes that "...the Spirit of Jesus would not allow them to" (Acts 16:7). It is very possible that at least one of the above messages from God came through words in somebody's mind.

Jesus hints to the disciples that He will put words into their minds when they need to share the Gospel: "Whenever you are arrested and brought to trial, do not worry beforehand about what to say. Just say whatever is given to you at the time, for it is not you speaking, but the Holy Spirit" (Mark 13:11). God told them not to prepare for their sermons under certain conditions, and that they were not to think up what to say in their minds with their own thoughts. Words "would be given" to them by the Spirit. I assume that means that God would put thoughts and words into their minds.

In Acts we see this in operation first-hand: "Then Peter, filled with the Holy Spirit, said to them..." (Acts 4:8). Again, "...Paul, filled with the Holy Spirit, looked straight at Elymas and said..." (Acts 13:9). There have been several occasions when I have sensed God's voice right before preaching, urging me not to use my prepared message. These sermons that I preached without notes were, as far as I could tell, as coherent and concise as my planned ones. The thoughts for each part of the message were in my mind when I needed them.

Jesus said, "...the Holy Spirit...will teach you all things and will remind you of everything I have said to you" (John 14: 26). The Spirit wants to communicate at times by putting thoughts into our mind, both pictures and words. The more we understand that He is seeking to do this, the more we will listen carefully to any "foreign" thoughts that are not ours. When we do, we will be guided in our service and encouraged in life.

CHAPTER 11:

INTUITION

Many Christians have been guided at one time or another by a strong, unexplained inner impulse that they ascribe to God. Even non-believers often speak of following what they call as "instinct" or a "gut feeling." These spiritual discernments often lead a person to the right place at the right time, unknowingly move them out of harm's way, or allow them to make the best decision when there is not enough information for a rational one. Most of these experiences are communications from a God who is constantly seeking our welfare and are also opportunities to use us to do His work. In this chapter and throughout this book that phenomenon will be termed "intuition."

Spiritual intuition is the ability of human beings to hear God's communication through their feelings. One's reason and intellect are uninvolved because the information received is impossible for the individual to know or learn naturally. It is supernaturally transmitted. I became aware of God speaking to me in this fashion, beginning five years ago. As God's written Word is the best guide for me in general matters of faith and life, intuition has become the most valuable guide in knowing what God wants me to do or where He wants me to go, both in my personal life and in my ministry.

SIMEON

Now there was a man in Jerusalem called Simeon, who was righteous and devout. He was waiting for the consolation of Israel, and the Holy Spirit was upon him. It had been revealed to him by the Holy

> *Spirit that he would not die before he had seen the Lord's Christ. Moved by the Spirit, he went into the temple courts. When the parents brought in the child Jesus to do for him what the custom of the Law required, Simeon took him in his arms and praised God, saying: "Sovereign Lord, as you have promised, you now dismiss your servant in peace. For my eyes have seen your salvation..." The child's father and mother marveled at what was said about him. Then Simeon blessed them and said to Mary, his mother: "This child is destined to cause the falling and rising of many in Israel, and to be a sign that will be spoken against, so that the thoughts of many hearts will be revealed. And a sword will pierce your own soul too."*
> Luke 2: 25-30, 33-35

One of the best examples of spiritual intuition in the Scriptures is found in Luke's account of the story of Simeon encountering the baby Jesus. Because Simeon was sensitive to the still small voice of the Holy Spirit, he was given the privilege of seeing and holding the Messiah, as well as uttering a prophetic blessing over Him.

In this story there are four examples of Simeon intuitively knowing something only because it was supernaturally communicated to him from God. Before these four, however, we read in Luke 2:26, "It had been revealed to him by the Holy Spirit that he would not die before he had seen the Lord's Christ." We are not told how God communicated this news to Simeon, whether through intuition, a dream, or some other means, but we immediately learn that Simeon was sensitive to God's voice.

The first example of Simeon's intuition is in Luke 2:27: "Moved by the Spirit, he went into the temple courts." Simeon was prompted to go somewhere specific at a particular time even though it does not appear that he knew why he was going. He simply obeyed the Spirit's voice within him. Here, intuition gave Simeon direction.

The second example is in Luke 2:27-28. Simeon was led by God to the temple courts, because at that moment Mary and Joseph had brought the baby Jesus there to consecrate Him to the Lord and to offer a sacrifice (Luke 2:22-23). When Simeon entered the courts there were, no doubt, numerous people milling around. Yet, Simeon, guided intuitively by the Spirit, went straight to Jesus and "...took him in his arms and praised God." This time, intuition gave Simeon discernment as to the presence of God in a certain place.

The third example is in Luke 2:29 when Simeon realized that God had fulfilled His promise: "Sovereign Lord, as you have promised, you now dismiss your servant in peace. For my eyes have seen your salvation ..." A peace fell over Simeon because he comprehended the work of God in his circumstances. He sensed that all things before him were working out according to God's divine plan, and he trusted that the Lord was in control. This complete peace came to him intuitively and was based on his faith in God's power to guide him.

The fourth example is in Luke 2:34-36. When prompted by God's Spirit, Simeon uttered prophetic words over the baby: "This child is destined to cause the falling and raising of many in Israel, and to be a sign that will be spoken against, so that the thoughts of many hearts will be revealed. And a sword will pierce your own soul too." Simeon uttered a prediction of the future that was given to him intuitively from the Holy Spirit concerning the God-ordained destiny of Jesus and his parents. Simeon had a glimpse into the future of this family.

Simeon intuitively heard the voice of God and it gave him direction, discernment, peace and a picture into the future of God's plan for certain individuals. All of these are still available to Christians today if they can learn how to activate their intuition. In the western world, this can be extremely difficult because reason has been overemphasized, in some cases excessively so. The idea that knowledge can come to an individual apart from the mind and reason is rarely even considered in our culture. Consequently, the Christian needs to make a deliberate attempt at rediscovering intuition, which can reveal knowledge that the person would never receive through reason alone. Intuitive knowledge is communicated supernaturally by the Almighty.

1. INTUITION COMMUNICATES DIRECTION

Since I have begun to listen to God through His still small voice, I have been astounded by how God positions me in the right place at the right time, often in an uncanny manner. The fruitfulness of my ministry as a pastor has been radically increased when I have become more sensitive to the promptings of the Spirit. I can do good ministry on my own, but when I am guided by the Lord's knowledge of people's needs and circumstances, it becomes great ministry. God has the best knowledge about who in my congregation needs what and when. God has a list of priorities that have His objectives in mind for my work. Since God knows all people perfectly and understands what every individual needs most, I am inclined to let Him give me direction in my pastoral activity. When I do this it feels less like me doing ministry and more like Jesus doing His ministry to people through me. I get the sense that He is back on earth doing His work by means of His Spirit guiding me to the places He wants to personally go. This has been evident in His call for me to minister and care for other pastors.

One of the first times I stepped out and acted upon an inner impulse was one day five years ago. As I was walking past the telephone in our kitchen, I had a subtle but clear sense that I was supposed to call a particular clergyman friend of mine who lives in a nearby community and whom I had not seen in months. I reached him at his church office and assumed that he was in need of something because God had put him on my heart. I asked him how he was doing. Though his response was not in depth, he shared honestly that things were not going well for him that morning. I could tell by his voice that it was more serious than simply a one-day concern. He was not interested in giving details over the phone at the time, but because I knew that he suffered regularly from depression, I assumed that might be his main issue. Before hanging up, I told him I would commit the next thirty minutes to praying for him.

A few days later I stopped by his office to see how he was doing. He shared with me that a few weeks before my call he had quit taking medication for his depression. The week of my call his depression was deepening daily, and the morning of my call he was sitting in his office, unable to properly function and do the work demanded of him. He had reached a low point and was agonizing over the question of whether or not he should restart his medication. He was encouraged by my call and thought that the timing was proof that God was present and wanted to guide him through the valley. After our conversation, he began to pray for wisdom concerning taking medication or not. In that prayer time, he intuitively sensed God encouraging him to get back on his meds, which he did.

Several years later, I ran into him at a local coffee house. He was alone, and since I had not seen or spoken with him in nearly six months, I was anxious to catch up. As we sat and talked I could tell that he was not himself. I asked him how he was doing on a scale from one to ten. He quickly replied, "Zero." He related that he was overcome with a profoundly debilitating depression. The amazing thing was what he said next: "I prayed this morning that I would run into you." We were both struck by how much God loved this man and actively sought to encourage him.

I began to speak a word of encouragement to my friend and it turned into a word from God. As I was talking, I began to intuitively know what to say. I instantly had a clear sense of what God wanted to speak to this man. One particular phrase pounded within my mind, and I knew it was what

God wanted to communicate more than anything else: "God is honored and pleased with you," I shared. I believe that that was exactly what this man needed to hear. I also sensed that I was supposed to tell him that God loved him very much and that he, for various reasons, was not able to believe that this good news was absolutely true for him.

I suggested that we go to his office to pray. I knew he had oil for anointing there. As he sat in a chair, I stood beside him and laid my hands on him to pray. I also anointed him with oil. When we had finished he had a calm, peaceful countenance. He said that, as we were in prayer, he had a distinct impression in his spirit of Jesus telling him simply, "I love you." It was thrilling to witness God speaking to somebody he loved and wonderfully exciting to be one of the means through which God spoke.

Another time I was on a spiritual retreat a couple of hours from home. As I was driving in my car, God placed a certain pastor on my heart. This man pastors a congregation in the same community as I, but we were mere acquaintances and had visited only on a couple of occasions. I had not seen him in many months and did not know anything about his personal life or his ministry. I just intuitively knew that I was supposed to skip lunch that day and instead fast and pray for him. A few days later, when I was back home and driving around town, I called him on my cell phone. I asked him how he was and he responded bluntly, "Terrible." We talked a little more and then I told him I would come to his church and pray with him right then. I did, and once again a pastor heard God saying, "I am thinking of you during your tough time."

During a birthday party at our home for my youngest son four years ago, I was standing off to the side watching David interact with friends on his big day. I suddenly realized that as my mind was focused on the party, I was silently praying for a pastor acquaintance of mine subconsciously. I had not purposely thought of this man, nor would my own mind have thought about him at that time. God put him on my heart because He wanted to speak a word to him. I continued to pray, and as I always do when God gives me a particular person to go see to pray for, assumed that this pastor was having a difficult time and God simply wanted to remind him that He was with him. I also instinctively knew that a particular issue was a problem.

The next day I felt compelled to go to his office and see him. Most times when I stopped by his church for one reason or another, he was out. As I drove to see him that day, I knew instinctively that he would be there. He was in his office when I arrived and he invited me in to visit. Because this happened in the first year of my practicing hearing God instinctively, and because this pastor belonged to a denomination that was most often wary of communication from God outside of the written word, I was a little nervous. What if there was nothing significantly wrong in his life? I would look like a fool and lose much credibility with this colleague if I told him that God told me to see him because he was going through a difficult time. I suddenly doubted whether the impulse was from God; but on the other hand, I did not want to risk disobeying Him. What made me question the word most was that this pastor was the most upbeat and positive fellow clergyman that I knew. He looked like he had no significant problems.

Gulping a time or two before beginning, I told him that God had put him on my heart the day before and led me to pray for him. I was candid and said that, although he did not appear to be troubled with anything at the present, I believed he was suffering in some deep way because God had brought him to my attention. I did not relate the one specific issue that I had sensed was a problem because I could not believe that it was true for him, and it would be an embarrassing issue to discuss if it was.

My colleague then shared that all was not right in his life. In fact, he began to recite a list of very serious problems that had all arisen in the previous months. One of the problems he mentioned was the issue I had sensed was a concern.

I then told him that the only reason that I could think of for God to give me that private information was that God wanted to remind him that He was very present, and wanted to take his hand and lead him through this difficult period. I believe that the man was encouraged by God through this word.

In ministry, I have been grateful that God has directed me more and more to the persons he wants to speak to at a particular time. One morning, as I was lying comfortably in bed and pondering the best way to spend my day off, I had an overwhelming sense that I was to go to the church office, which was twenty miles north of our home. I knew that this impulse was from God because it was something that I never would have thought of or felt on my own. In fact, it was diametrically opposed to my own desires.

At first, I was extremely disappointed, so much so that I looked toward the ceiling and asked, "Lord, is this impulse from You? Do You really want me to go to the church?" When I asked, I knew that He was confirming that it was Him directing me. Like Simeon, I went off to the temple courts, not knowing what I was to do there. Since I did not get a sense that I was to do any particular office work, I brought a writing project with me. All I had heard was that I was to go to the office. When I arrived I unlocked the outside door and then went to the hiding place where the key to the offices were. I did not carry an office key with me. I was surprised to discover that the key was missing and I stood outside my office for a few minutes, contemplating what to do next. Since I strongly believed that God had directed me there, and I knew that He knew the key was gone, I trusted that He had another task in mind for me. I decided to call the church secretary from the phone that was in the kitchen to see if I could get a key from her. She happened to be home and suggested that her son drive the key to the Dairy Queen in the nearest town, which was seven miles away. I drove further north and was now twenty-seven miles from home on my day off, and wondering what God was up to.

This all took place on a Monday. I had planned to drive to this very town the following day to visit a dozen members of our congregation who lived in two nursing homes there. Since I was already in town, I decided to save some time and make the visits that day, since I did not hear anything else specific from the Lord. The first person I visited was an elderly woman named Marie. The moment I entered her room, I knew why the Lord had guided me there. Oxygen tubes were in her nose and a red rose was laying on a Bible that was placed by Marie's head on the pillow. I knew instantly that she was dying. Marie's eyes were closed and she was unresponsive. A nurse told me that they had just begun giving her morphine and were expecting her to die at any time. I was surprised when I learned that Marie had quit eating three days before, and from that moment had begun a serious decline. I was terribly disappointed that a member of my congregation was dying and I had not been contacted. I prayed with Marie and read Scripture to her. I committed her to the Lord and said a benediction over her.

As I drove home, I was sure that Marie would die before the next afternoon, the time I had originally scheduled to visit the nursing home to see her. I concluded that God stirred me on my day off to this task because the next day would have been too late. I can not adequately convey to the reader how great a gift it was to me that I was able to spend that time with a member I cared about, and wanted to care for in the best possible way, especially at such a crucial moment. I knew that God had honored Marie's deep faith, and that she would want a pastor to give her a final benediction. Also, God knew that much of her family was unchurched and that I would gain honor and respect in their eyes if I had been there in their mother's darkest hour. If I had not gone to see her during the four days when she was dying, her family could easily have assumed that the church had failed them, giving them another reason to stay away from institutionalized religion.

Intuition has also been a way by which God has directed me in personal matters. Last June was the first-ever Groethe reunion in Hemsedal, Norway. My father had been doing most of the planning, along with his brother; the endeavor had taken three years. I was excited about going, mostly because

I wanted to be with my father as I saw the family birthplace for the first time. I obtained my visa and had arranged to take two weeks off from work to attend the reunion. My father, my brother Craig and I began to make more specific plans a few months before the departure date. We planned our housing, decided which expenses to share, and made a list of what items we would want to bring along. I had the money in the bank for the trip and had paid a $100 deposit on my airline ticket.

In May, I began to sense that I shouldn't go. I believed that it was God's voice telling me to stay home. I procrastinated in telling my father because I knew how disappointed he would be, but had to do it before I paid the balance of the air fare. He did not understand at first, of course, but I sheepishly told him that I believed that God was encouraging me to cancel. It was difficult for me to do this, but I was convinced that the direction was from the Lord. As the departure day drew closer, I mused with some Christian friends as to why I would be kept in the States, and wondered if I would ever discern God's intentions in the matter.

The answer came pointedly a week before the trip. My father had a test done at a Fargo hospital to check the condition of his heart, merely as a precaution. The tests showed serious damage, however, and my father was immediately rushed into the operating room where he had double by-pass surgery. My father had weeks of recovery ahead of him and the Norway trip was out of the question. My wife and I had just finished an addition to our house and because of a variety of circumstances, it was best for my parents to stay with us as he recovered. Craig also canceled the Norway trip for himself and his three children. As a result, he faced very irritating and costly limitations on his future use or refund of the tickets. God saved me time, energy, and money while deepening my trust in His ability to know what's best for me.

Help for even simple things can come through intuition. For example, I finished my office work one evening and locked my office door on my way out to my car. As I headed down the hallway toward the entrance, I passed a closed door which led to our congregation's conference room/library. I stopped suddenly in my tracks because I had a strange inclination to go into the room. I felt a little silly as I did because I could not imagine why God would have me do so. I saw nothing unusual as I walked across the room but went the entire length of it anyway. I had just begun to pastor there, and had previously noticed a small room off to the side in the back. When I entered it, I found the room contained a sink and a cabinet. On the cabinet was a coffee maker with a glass coffee pot sitting on the burner. I immediately noticed that a red light was on and felt the burner. It was hot. The liquid in the glass pot had long since evaporated and the bottom was turning charcoal black.

What would have happened if I had not spotted it? I am not certain, but I suspect that God had a reason. I have discovered that God cares about the smallest pieces of life, and that it could have simply resulted in a ruined coffee pot if I had not seen it. I do know that nobody would have been in the church for at least three days because it was a country church with a part-time secretary. If nothing else, God was interested in helping me practice hearing His voice and obeying.

2. INTUITION GIVES DISCERNMENT

In the temple courts, Simeon was able to identify the presence of Jesus among the many other people present. He was guided by means of intuition. When intuition is used to distinguish whether the flesh, a demonic force, or God is the primary presence in an individual or circumstance, it is called discernment. By means of this helpful tool, Christians can know whether to embrace a person or an event, or to be cautious because a force other than God is at work.

Simeon discerned where Jesus was in the temple because God communicated to him through intuition. In Luke 1:41, Mary, who was pregnant with Jesus, went to visit her relative Elizabeth, who was pregnant with John. When the two women met, John leaped in Elizabeth's womb and then she was filled with the Holy Spirit. She was intuitively given knowledge by God that the baby in Mary's womb was her "Lord." Elizabeth, in other words, discerned the presence of God in front of her as she was given the supernatural ability to do so.

Like Elizabeth, all Christians have the ability to know where Jesus is working in the world around them or to know if He is present in another person. Believers have God's Spirit living within their spirits, and when in the presence of Christ somewhere outside themselves, there can be a sort of "leap" of the spirit within them, like John in Elizabeth, that communicates where Jesus is.

Two summers ago, my wife and I spent a morning going to garage sales. As we browsed through used items in one particular garage, I had an overpowering feeling of Jesus' presence in that place. It was as if God's Spirit within me jumped to indicate that fact. I told the man and woman who owned the house that I sensed the Holy Spirit strongly at their place and I said that I assumed that they were active followers of Christ. They were surprised that I said what I did, but quickly confirmed that Jesus was the center of their lives. We talked awhile and their passionate love for God came through clearly.

Spiritual discernment gives the believer the ability to sense Jesus in circumstances as well as in people. If this occurs we can know where He is working and join Him. The constant worry for me as an interim pastor is that when the church I temporarily serve finds a new pastor and doesn't need me anymore, I have a month to find another church in a forty-mile radius (my criteria) that is just then losing their pastor and almost ready for an interim. I began interim ministry only because my denomination was confident that I could remain employed consistently in the area to which my family chose to move. But after my first assignment was close to being completed, the church headquarters informed me that not only was there no congregation nearby who presently needed an interim, they could see no openings in the distant future.

Within a few weeks of my employment being terminated I received a call from a lay leader of the Presbyterian/UCC congregation that was only two blocks away on the same street as the church I served. The woman said that they had just lost their pastor and were in need of an interim. Would I be interested? I was jubilant that God had found me a job possibility. I responded affirmatively. She called a few days later, however, and informed me that they had found a Presbyterian interim pastor from another state that they had interviewed and decided to hire. I was disappointed that the only possibility of employment that I knew of had just fallen through. We exchanged pleasantries, and then ended our conversation. As I hung up the phone, I had the overwhelming feeling that I would be their interim. At first I argued with God asking how that was possible, but finally I simply passively believed that He was at work. That knowledge kept me from unnecessary stress and anxiety that I would have otherwise felt, because I knew that God would provide. I was not surprised when the same woman called a week later and said that the other interim was now unable to come. Was I still interested? I met with the council, was hired, and began what turned into a fourteen-month interim that provided some of the most satisfying and enjoyable ministry I have ever experienced. Knowing that it was God's plan for me to be at that church at that time accomplished two things: first, it saved me the week-long worry I would have had if I had not believed God was providing for me, and secondly, I felt a strong confidence that during my entire stay there, I was exactly where God wanted me. I sensed Jesus in that situation and jumped in after him.

God can also communicate to our feelings (intuition) that a person or activity carries the presence and blessing of Jesus. We should be able to discern if human ambition or demonic influence controls a person or event. I remember about a dozen experiences where I have known a particular person and have felt an awkward, negative feeling concerning them, even though they appeared to be normal and healthy in their faith. It has been uncanny how these intuitive clues about someone's spiritual condition have proven true. Many times I have refrained from putting someone into a leadership position in the church because of these impressions. In every case, I eventually learned why it would have been harmful to do so. I regret, however, that more often than not I am unable to discern an ungodly situation and have made many mistakes as a result.

The Holy Spirit can also help us to discern when something is human-initiated or motivated. This is important because we so often mistake our own enthusiasm or ideas as the Spirit's. Consequently, we make decisions or do things in the flesh without the Spirit's endorsement, with results that may be mixed and relatively unproductive in the Kingdom of God.

When it is especially difficult to discern whether your plans or ideas are flesh or Spirit, you may want to wait as long as possible to decide because human enthusiasm fades and dies over time, but Spirit-motivated things will not only keep their passion, but will strengthen in conviction.

3. INTUITION COMPREHENDS THE PRESENCE OF GOD THROUGH PEACE

Simeon was ready to die because he had experienced the peace of knowing God's presence in the baby Jesus. That peace was the certainty that God was in control of the affairs surrounding Simeon's life. The old man saw only a helpless baby with his eyes, but God communicated to his feelings a sense of profound hope because of what God was working for good in that tiny person.

Probably the sweetest communication of God's Spirit is the incomprehensible wonder of His divine peace that He bestows at the least-imaginable times and places. That peace is the intuitive recognition of God's holy presence. When anyone feels that peace, it is his intuitive sense that God is near and working His purposes in spite of all evidence to the contrary.

When I was in my first year of ministry, I soon became overwhelmed with stress when work piled up for the first time. I developed a numbing sensation in my sternum because of it. I became frazzled and extremely tense. I could not imagine doing what lay before me. As I prayed in the midst of it, a peace descended upon me that revealed God's presence and His activity in my affairs. Like Simeon, I knew that everything was being taken care of. My numbness departed and I found a calm that carried me through the days after with an unexpected tranquility.

The stories of people I know or of whom I have pastored who have received this indescribable sense of peace in periods of fear and deep anxiety are too many to recount here. Christians have felt it during severe trials, in times of great grief, in moments of overpowering fear, and when confusion blocks all reason. When it comes, it so contradicts one's own feelings at the time that it is immediately recognized as the presence of God. Simeon discerned God bringing about the salvation of the world through His power when he looked at a weak child who could do nothing. The peace that envelops people today allows them also to look at worrisome circumstances and discern that God will work them all out for His glory.

4. INTUITION HELPS US KNOW THE DESTINY OF INDIVIDUALS OR COMMUNITIES

At the conclusion of Simeon's encounter with Jesus, he speaks prophetic words over the baby and parents. He intuitively receives this knowledge from the Lord so that he can encourage Mary and Joseph and help prepare them for what lay ahead. He claimed that Jesus would one day cause the rise and fall of many individuals and reveal people's hearts. This declaration is a general description of God's destiny for His son. It also declares God's destiny for the people of Israel: they will have a Savior who will challenge and judge their lives. He also gives hints of Mary and Joseph's destiny; because of the suffering of the Messiah, they would face suffering as well.

A clergy friend of mine took a new call several states away from his old position. After he had been at the new congregation awhile, he had dream one night in which he was asked to speak at an annual Lutheran gathering in his former district. In his dream he saw and heard himself give the message. He was not totally surprised, then, when he got a call from his former district, and was asked if he would speak at the event about which he had dreamed. He preached the sermon from his dream and it was a powerful message. He knew ahead of time God's plan for him.

The above story deals with a one-time experience and a calling by God to perform a certain task. Many times, however, God gives individuals an intuitive understanding of what career or ministry He has in store for them. Knowing where God is leading causes one to feel relaxed about the present.

On a number of occasions, I have had an intuitive sense of another Christian's destiny (ultimate calling of God). One good friend of mine has been a parish pastor for many years. He is very gifted at it. He also has great teaching gifts and a passion in that area, but he has usually down-played the possibility of leaving parish ministry for teaching. I had a very strong intuitive sense that he would leave the congregational ministry and teach. I knew it was God's destiny for him, but was hesitant to be bold about telling him because he did not think that he was necessarily heading in that direction. A few months ago, he received a call to teach at his denomination's seminary.

God can give us knowledge of His destiny for a congregation as well. At the church I presently serve, it was almost unanimous among the leadership that we were to build a new building, even though we would be hard-pressed to pay for it. One mature Christian woman had been out for a walk in the neighborhood years before and as she passed the church, God gave her a vision of a new building on the same site on the other side of the lot. We are now in the process of building it. It is being erected on the same spot and facing the same direction as that woman's vision. She did not share this dream publicly until recently. She, along with most of the leadership of the church, has had a strong impression that building is God's destiny for us at this time.

God can communicate with us through our feelings (intuition). It is often difficult for us to allow this to happen because we know how fickle and unreliable our feelings can be. But ultimately, the more we can distinguish between out natural feelings and those that are foreign to us (God's voice), the more beneficial and trustworthy hearing God's voice intuitively can be. God can guide, instruct, comfort, and lead us into ministry opportunities through intuition.

CHAPTER 12:

DREAMS

Even though God frequently communicated through dreams and visions to people in both the Old and New Testaments, the church today has all but abandoned the notion that He continues to do so. This isn't surprising for a culture that emphasizes reason, while being suspicious of truth being communicated through irrational means. Dreams and visions are two of these irrational experiences. While visions are given when one is awake, dreams are received when in the unconscious state of sleep.

For the first twelve years of my ministry as a pastor, I never even considered dreams as a possible vehicle for God's communication. I now find that surprising because of the wonderful benefits dreams have had for many whose stories are related in the Bible. Dreams are one of the most accessible and profitable ways to get a direct word from God, yet we continue to leave this arena totally unexplored and unexploited. Since I have taken dreams seriously, I am now a convicted believer in the power they often have for putting us in touch with God's word and will for our lives at a personal level. In just the past two years I have witnessed many examples where dreams have profoundly guided, comforted and encouraged individuals. I have also heard of dreams that accurately predicted the future, or that protected a person, or showed them what to do in a particular situation. These have all been examples of the truth that God loves to speak with His people and how He desperately desires to help us on our journey.

Dreams were one of the most common methods God used to communicate to people in the 1500-year period between Abraham and the Apostle Paul. An interesting element of these Biblical accounts is that God sent dreams to many non-believers as well. In fact, one of the first examples of dreams in the Old Testament is given to a heathen king, Abimelech, in order to keep him from sinning (Gen. 20:1-7). When Abraham and Sarah were visiting his territory, Abraham deceived the locals by saying that his wife was his sister, although that was technically not a lie. Because of the deception, Abimelech took Sarah as one of his women. God visited Abimelech in a dream and informed the king that Sarah was a married woman. Although God was certainly protecting His assets by guarding the family He had called as his ambassadors, He was also very interested in the welfare of this unbelieving king. Abimelech was quick to right the wrong he had unintentionally committed by returning Sarah safely back to her husband. God then spoke in another dream (Gen 20:6-7) to the king and acknowledged that he had done this with a clear conscience. God admits that He saved Abimelech because he was innocent.

At Bethel, Jacob saw his now famous dream of the ladder from heaven to earth (Gen. 28:10-15). God stood above the top of the ladder and restated the call He had issued Abraham and promised to take care of Jacob as he traveled to and from Paddan Aram. Jacob's son Joseph was the classic dreamer and dream interpreter. As a boy he had a dream that showed his future destiny as ruling over his family. When in an Egyptian prison, Joseph heard dreams from two former officials of Pharaoh (Gen. 40). Each dream revealed the dreamer's destiny. One was to be released from prison and reinstated to his old position, while the other one was to be executed. Finally, Pharaoh had two dreams (Gen. 41) that accurately predicted seven years of good crops followed by seven years of famine. God provided valuable information that in the end saved thousands of lives, including Jacob's own family in Canaan.

When the Israelite army was encamped against the army of Midian, Gideon was unsure if he should attack the next morning or stay where he was. The Lord instructed Gideon to sneak up on the enemy camp during the night with his servant, where he would hear something that would convince him what to do. What Gideon overheard in his eavesdropping was a Midianite private sharing his dream with a friend (Judges 7:9-17). In the dream "a round loaf of barley bread came tumbling into the Midianite camp" and slammed into the tent, destroying it. The friend correctly interpreted the dream to mean that Gideon and his smaller army would defeat the Midianites. Gideon was convinced that the dream was of God, and it was enough to encourage him to mount an attack which resulted in a rout of the Midianite army.

When the Lord appeared to Solomon to grant him one wish, he did so in a dream (I Kings 3:4). Job also understood that God spoke in dreams:

Dreams

> *...God does speak—now one way, now another—though man may not perceive it. In a dream, in a vision of the night, when deep sleep falls on men as thy slumber in their beds, he may speak in their ears and terrify them with warnings, to turn man from wrongdoing and keep him from pride, to preserve his soul from the pit.*
>
> Job 33:14-18a

Most of the messages of the prophets were delivered to them in dreams and visions. In Numbers, the Lord himself said, *"When a prophet of the Lord is among you, I reveal myself to him in visions, I speak to him in dreams"* (Numbers 12:6).

The prophetic books of Daniel and Ezekiel are full of dreams. In Daniel, the foreign king Nebuchadnezzar had dreams, interpreted by Daniel, which foretold the king's insanity. Daniel himself had a couple of dreams that spoke about the fate of several nations. Ezekiel's most famous dream, which he had when he was in exile in Babylonia with the Hebrew people, was of the valley of dry bones which miraculously came to life. This dream gave hope to the exiles, many of whom had despaired of any hope.

In the New Testament, dreams appear quickly in the second chapter of Matthew. This time it was to another Joseph, Mary's betrothed. An angel appeared to him in a dream and warned him of Herod's intent to find the baby Jesus and kill him. He was instructed to flee to Egypt and wait there until God told him something different. After Herod died, an angel again appeared to Joseph in a dream and instructed him to return to Israel.

In Acts 2, on the evening of Pentecost when the followers of the ascended Jesus were filled with the Holy Spirit, Peter quoted Joel:

> *'In the last days, God says, I will pour out my Spirit on all people. Your sons and daughters will prophecy, your young men will see visions, your old men will dream dreams.'*
>
> Acts 2:17 (Joel 2:28)

Also in Acts (chapter 10), the God-fearing Gentile Cornelius had a vision where an angel told him to send men to search for a man named Peter in Joppa and bring him to Cornelius' house. At the same time, Peter had his housetop vision through which God taught him that there should be no distinctions between Gentiles and Jews. These two visions are what brought Peter and Cornelius together. As a result, Cornelius' entire household came to believe in Jesus Christ. Also in Acts, Paul had a dream that directed him to Macedonia (Acts 16:6-10), where Jesus wanted him to preach the Gospel. Finally, the entire book of Revelation is a fantastic vision where God takes John to heaven, showing him hints of the future of the Church in the world.

Dreams from God can accomplish many things, but I think most can be fit into one of four general categories: 1) warning dreams; 2) dreams that convey important information; 3) dreams that declare an individual's or a community's destiny; and 4) dreams that comfort. The following are present-day dreams that have accomplished each of the above four purposes.

1. DREAMS AND VISIONS WARN OF IMPENDING DANGER

A dream saved Abimelech from sinning and prevented a curse from falling on his household. Another dream warned Joseph and Mary of imminent danger and saved Jesus' life. Both of these were warning dreams in which God communicated the knowledge of impending danger. He does the same today.

Several years ago, my brother Craig had a dream that vividly showed his children driving a car and having a serious accident. When he awoke, he wrote his dream down, as he always does. He knew that the dream was from God, but he also knew that most images in dreams are usually symbolic and metaphorical, not literal. But as he prayed about it, he had a clear sense that it was, in fact, an accurate picture of upcoming danger for his three children. Craig records every detail he remembers of his dreams, but when he came to describing the road on which the car was traveling, he was unsure if it was a two-lane or four-lane. He wrote down this uncertainty in his journal.

Craig first did what we all should do when receiving dreams that seem to say that somebody is in danger. He prayed. He asked God to protect his children, especially on the road. That evening, less than twenty-four hours after his prayer, his three children were returning home from a concert in a town a couple of hours away. The kids were in two different vehicles, with several friends along in each car. His daughter was driving the lead vehicle while his son, Carey, followed behind in the second. It was dark.

At one point, Carey decided to pass the other car, so he moved to the left lane and began to gain on the other vehicle. As he was driving, Carey was deeply engaged in a conversation with a friend and was not fully concentrating on the road. There was a frontage road alongside this two-lane highway and Carey mistakenly assumed that the frontage road was the other two lanes of the four-lane highway. As he continued to engage in serious conversation with the person in the passenger seat, Carey assumed that the oncoming headlights were from cars that were not in his passing lane but were in their own two lanes, so he took his time passing. If Carey had continued on his course, his car would have collided with the first vehicle coming at him. Carey became aware of the danger only at the last moment, and barely swerved out of the way before an accident occurred. When our niece, who had been driving the lead car, comprehended the serious danger to the other car, she panicked. She understood immediately how serious the problem was.

Did Craig's dream and following prayer prevent an accident, and perhaps save lives? Our family is certain of it. The odds of the dream and near accident happening the same day are too highly improbable to be a coincidence. In the seven thousand days that my brother has had at least one child, this warning dream was the only one of such serious nature that Craig had ever had. The near-accident was the closest those young people had ever been to serious injury and the threat of death in the tens of thousands of miles that they had previously driven in a car. It is clear to us that God shared this information with Craig so that he could pray for this specific threat of danger, and thus be a part of preventing it.

Craig is a modern-day dreamer like Joseph in the Old Testament, as well as an interpreter of other people's dreams that are given to them by the Lord. After much study and experience, along with spiritual intuition, he has come to understand much of what the dreams God gives to specific individuals mean. Consequently, he receives hundreds of phone calls and e-mails every year from people about their dreams. I do not have time here to share the amazing fruit that has come from listening to these dreams, but many people have been guided and comforted in profound ways.

On September 24, 2003, Craig called a married couple who were friends of his and said that he was stopping by their home for coffee and a visit. While they were chatting, the wife, Theresa, asked Craig if dates were significant when they appeared in dreams. She went on to share a dream she had had two weeks previously. In the dream she was in a living room sitting on a couch. The room had pale blue walls and they were unusually high. All of a sudden, a bald man with a mustache burst into the room holding a boy in both arms. The boy had an injury to his leg and the man was looking for a doctor to help. He gave Theresa a piece of paper with an appointment date on it. She could not make out anything on the paper, except at the bottom of the paper the date "September 24, 2003" was clearly visible.

Craig concluded that two people, who were unknown to them, were in some kind of danger. Because the date in the dream was that day, he suggested that they pray immediately. They interceded for the injured boy by placing him into the hands of the Lord. They covered the situation that this dream represented with prayer and asked God to prevent or minimize the harm done whatever situation was ahead. They prayed for angels to surround the people involved in the event, and to protect and guard them.

At the same time that this conversation between Craig and Theresa began, Theresa's husband received a call on his cell phone and went off to answer it. The next day they checked the call log on the phone and discovered that the call was received at 11:17 am. After visiting a bit longer, Craig left for a lunch engagement at a local restaurant. He ate and when he was at the till paying, the owner of the restaurant excitedly asked, "Have you heard about the shootings?" Craig had not. She said that at the Rocori high school, about twenty miles away, a student had shot two other kids.

As Craig was leaving the restaurant, he passed the doorway that led to the bar. When he looked inside, a TV was on and there was a picture of a bald man with a mustache. Craig immediately thought of the man in the dream. The man was the school's physical education teacher who had been present during the shootings. In fact, the shootings took place in the gym as students for his next class were beginning to filter in. After two students were shot (one died immediately and the other died later at the hospital), the teacher faced the student who had the gun and held his hand out while shouting "Stop!" The boy eventually dropped the gun and the teacher grabbed him and escorted him away.

What difference did the dream and the praying make? Two students were killed. Did the intercession prevent further deaths and injuries? Did it protect the teacher? Did it help to cause the young man to drop the gun, or to keep him from shooting himself? We will never know on this side of eternity. My conclusion is that the prayers did accomplish something profound, probably preventing the shooting of more people and providing protection for the teacher. We assume this because Craig coincidentally stopped by the house of the woman with the dream on the morning that the incident took place. She would not have called him that day. The dream had a date referring to that very day, and it led them to pray for a bald man and for a situation where there would be the danger of boys being hurt. Also, the shooting took place at 1:41, twenty-four minutes after Craig and Theresa prayed. Coincidence? I don't think so.

Let me make this incident even more incredible. The evening of the shootings a Christian acquaintance stopped by Craig's house because he wanted to share something. He came because he knew that Craig had a ministry with dreams. This man's son was a student at Rocori high school, where the shootings took place. He shared that a couple of years previous to that day, his son had a dream in which a boy at school pointed a gun at him. He simply turned the gun in the other direction, facing away from himself. Then, the night before the shootings, his son's girlfriend had a dream. In it, her boyfriend was shot by another student at school and killed. The following morning, the boy went to the boy's locker room to dress for his gym class. A friend of his had done something to his locker as a practical joke so that it would not open. Because of the delay in getting his locker open, the boy was still in the locker room when he heard the shootings in the gym.

Added to this, another acquaintance of Craig's, a Christian woman, told Craig an interesting incident. This woman usually goes to sleep with the TV on and it automatically shuts off within half an hour. The night (or early morning) before the shootings, she was shocked out of sleep, hearing a pounding on a door and a policeman's voice shouting, "Let us in!" She calmed down when she realized that it was a program on her television which, for some reason, had not shut off on its own. She had a sense that this may all have happened to get her up to pray for someone who was about to be in danger. She prayed generally for protection about anyone that the dream might be referring to.

God warns people today through dreams, but we, most likely, miss a great majority of them. Most dreams are symbolic, not literal, but a good rule of thumb for Christians who have dreams in which somebody is harmed or in possible danger is to pray fervently for that individual or individuals. Pray that God's angels would protect whoever is in trouble. Pray that any harm that would naturally come to the person(s) in the dream would be averted. It may also be helpful to ask God to give you a better idea of who and what to pray for through an intuitive word or a thought or picture in the mind and then sit quietly before God for direction. If none comes, then pray generally for whatever the dream might be referring to.

2. DREAMS AND VISIONS CAN PROVIDE VALUABLE INFORMATION

My daughter Kim, who is in high school, shared a dream with my wife and me a few months ago. In the dream, she was in a large outdoor pool with a friend of hers. There was a stiff wind and it was creating large waves in the pool which pushed Kim and her friend first to one side and then to the other. In the middle of the pool was a platform upon which stood a high-school-age girl. It was victory platform and the girl had a first-place trophy.

Kim suddenly wanted to get out of the pool, but the sides were so slippery that she could not manage on her own. Then she noticed a Christian friend at the edge of the pool waiting to help her out. With her aid, Kim was able to get out of the pool.

My daughter had a strong sense that the dream was a word from God. I agreed. As we thought about possible interpretations, God slowly revealed to me the meaning. I intuitively knew that our final conclusions concerning the dream were of God. Water so often refers to the Holy Spirit but can also symbolize the human spirit (apart from God) or maybe even demonic spirits. In this case, the particular friend who was in the pool was not a Christian. Of all of Kim's friends, she is the most worldly, that is, she makes decisions with no thought for God's will. My wife remarked that she is a "free spirit," meaning not anchored morally. The pool symbolized the unredeemed human spirit that is tossed to and fro because it has no moral grounding. Kim was in the pool because she is attracted to that free spirit of her friend. The girl with the trophy in the middle of the pool represented the lure of that lifestyle. If Kim lived there, she would be much more popular than if she continued to follow Christ, held fast to a moral code and devoted herself to serving God, things which would not win Kim a first-place trophy in the eyes of her peers.

I warned Kim to be careful when choosing who she would spend most of her time with, and explained about the dangers of hanging out with non-Christians with few morals. I explained that our peers exercise much more influence on us than we imagine, for good or for evil. I quoted from James 1:6, "He who doubts is like a wave of the sea, blown and tossed by the wind." I encouraged her to nurture her relationships with her Christian friends, who are out of the pool, and they would help steer her right.

It was late, so I went to bed after our discussion. Kim, being a night owl, was up for an hour or two longer. She went to her bedroom where she read two things: her teen devotional and her Bible, which is designed for teenage girls and written in contemporary terms. The devotion for the day talked about the possible harmful influences of friends who are not Christians and warned readers to be careful not to be influenced away from Christian principles by them. The Bible passage to which she turned unintentionally was the same James passage that I had quoted.

God convinced Kim that it was His voice speaking to her. He did it first through her dream, then through the spiritual discernment of her father, and finally through coincidence when the first two items she read after our talk had the identical message as the one I had discerned from the dream. God gave Kim helpful information that may, in the end, save her from much pain and trouble.

This past year, the local media of Seattle as well as the national media shared with the country a dream that saved a young woman's life. A seventeen-year-old high school student was reported missing after she left a party in a Seattle suburb. Police were not sure if she ran away, had an accident, or was kidnapped. For seven days, hundreds of people looked for clues of her whereabouts. When police learned that she had been at a party, they searched the probable routes home from that location. Nothing was found.

After the seventh day, a woman who was a member of the church that the missing girl's family attended had two dreams. In the dreams, she saw a car that had smashed into trees at the bottom of a steep hill. She also received information about the general location of where the car went off the road. She had been praying for the girl and immediately understood that the dream was giving directions to her.

The next day the woman and her daughter went for a drive in the Seattle suburbs, in hopes that the dream was going to lead her to the girl. It was not long before she stopped at the side of the road at a place that seemed familiar to her from the dream. She walked through trees and heavy underbrush down a steep embankment, looking for some sign of a car. In her dream, she had walked through some heavy woods. She was about to stop when she heard the words, "Keep going. Keep going." The woman's daughter stood on top of the hill and encouraged her to continue onward through the heavy foliage. She suddenly came upon a car that had crashed into trees. Inside was the missing young woman. She was injured with various broken bones and had a blot clot, but she was alive.

Imagine how many times God may be communicating valuable information to us through dreams, but it goes unheeded because we do not believe that God does this sort of thing. In the above story, a person's life was saved. Think of what God might be able to do through us if we listened more carefully.

I categorize "giving information" as a separate function of dreams, even though warning dreams consist of valuable information given to one who can alter upcoming events through prayer or exercising caution. Also, our next category, "Dreams reveal a person's destiny," is actually the giving of information concerning what God desires a person to be or do with her life. The distinctions I want to make here are these: *warning* dreams give information about future events that could cause harm, while dreams that reveal one's God desired destiny simply give *information* about what God's call is upon one's life. The category of dreams I describe as information-sharing most often give insight into present realities, helping one to make a good decision or to learn something that leads to better service to others.

One woman in the church I presently serve lost the diamond from her wedding ring. She noticed it was missing about mid-morning on a Saturday after spending several hours doing miscellaneous chores. She spent hours looking for it without success. She was so grieved that she offered up several prayers asking God to help her find it. In a dream, she was looking through the garbage bag in her house and found the diamond in an empty egg carton. When she woke up, she looked in the garbage bag and found an egg carton. When she checked inside nothing was there. Next to the carton was a brownie box that was now stuffed with scrap paper. Inside she found the diamond. She would never have thought of looking there if it were not for the dream. God gave her information that only He knew.

A high-school-age young man from the town in which I live has a Christian mother and a Muslim father. His parents are divorced. He lives with his mother in Minnesota most of the time but spends a couple of months every summer in the state of Washington with his father. Several Christian friends of this young man shared Christ with him in the last two years, and he gave his life to the Lord. He is growing in faith steadily and a number of young men have taken it upon themselves to mentor him.

One summer recently, when the boy was with his father in Washington, two of his Minnesota Christian friends decided to drive out to see him, making a vacation out of the trip. The boy was thrilled at the idea of their visit, but his father quickly quenched his joy by forbidding his son to see any Christian friends while he stayed with him. His young Christian friends were also disappointed, but they began to pray that God would change the father's mind. One of the men prayed specifically that the dad would receive a dream to that affect. He did. In it he saw God and Jesus standing together, ordering him to allow his son to see those Christian friends. Needless to say, he did. The dream gave the man important information from God.

3. DREAMS AND VISIONS CAN REVEAL OR CONFIRM GOD'S DESTINIES FOR INDIVIDUALS OR COMMUNITIES

God had a specific purpose for Abraham and Sarah. In chapter twelve of Genesis, we eavesdrop on the divine call to this couple: "I will make you into a great nation and I will bless you; I will make your name great, and you will be a blessing. I will bless those who bless you, and whoever curses you I will curse; and all the peoples on earth will be blessed through you" (Genesis 12:2-3). God's plan was to use this family to lead all the nations of the world back into a relationship with himself. This was the destiny that God envisioned for them.

It was a tall order for two ordinary people, especially because they were past their prime and Sarah could not bear children. Because the task was not only incredible but impossible, Abraham and Sarah had a difficult time believing it. That is why God continued to reassure them that it was true. In Genesis 15:1-16, God encounters a skeptical Abraham in a vision in order to encourage him to believe what God said he would do through him. Abraham comes clean with his doubt when he said, "O Sovereign Lord, what can you give me since I remain childless...You have given me no children." What follows is a reiteration of God's original call and an attempt to convince Abraham that He would bring it about.

It was in a dream that God spoke to Jacob at Bethel in order to reiterate the destiny God wanted his family to fulfill, as well as His destiny for the nation of Israel. It was similar to God's original call to Abraham.

God shared the destiny He had in mind for Joseph with him in dreams while he was still a boy. The dreams spoke of Joseph's destiny as being the leader of his family at some future date, although he was the second youngest son. Many years later, when he was the head of agriculture in Egypt, he saved his family because of his leadership position. Joseph also interpreted the dreams of two fellow prisoners when he was locked up unjustly. The future destiny of each man was revealed; one would be executed and the other would be re-instated as the cup-bearer for the king (Genesis 40:1-12).

Most of the words that the prophets heard from God came from visions and dreams (Numbers 12:6). One of the common proclamations they gave was to communicate Israel's God-desired destiny. Isaiah 49:6 is a good example: "...It is too small a thing for you to be my servants to restore the tribes of Jacob and bring back those of Israel I have kept. I will also make you a light for the Gentiles, that you may bring my salvation to the ends of the earth." God had a specific destiny for Israel and it involved, as His call always does, a commission to serve Him by helping others.

God continues to speak personally to both individuals and communities of faith in order to share His vision of the great things He wants them to do for Him. The Scriptures communicate a general idea of God's call to all believers (e.g. care for the poor and weak, share Christ with the lost, love enemies, etc.), but God has a specific plan for each individual that He wants to communicate personally. One way He does this is by creating us with certain talents and convictions through which He give us hints as to what God wants to do with us. Another way He accomplishes the sharing of His vision for our service is through dreams.

A faithful member of the congregation I now serve is a retired teacher. When she was a high school student in the 1940s, she felt a call to teach, but thought it was impossible because her family could not afford to send her to college. One night she had a dream that led her to look up a particular chapter in the New Testament. In the text Jesus was giving a teaching to His disciples about how nothing is impossible with God. She believed that God was encouraging her to continue to pursue a teaching degree. She did and eventually went to college, graduated, and spent a lifetime in the classroom. God confirmed her inner inclinations that the destiny He desired for her was teaching.

A friend of mine who serves a nearby parish as pastor went into ministry in response to a dream. A young man who grew up in the church I now serve, but who currently lives elsewhere, visited a worship service recently. He came into my office to introduce himself before the service began. He shared details about his ungodly past, which included drugs and witchcraft. Because of a dream he received from the Lord, he escaped his dangerous lifestyle and gave his life to Christ. In the past three months, three leaders of my congregation have shared dreams with me revealing more clearly what God's plan of service for each of them is. The direction given in each dream was relevant and extremely helpful.

God has great plans to use you in ways that are beyond what you can imagine. That is why so few of us are actually fulfilling the destiny to which He calls us. It is also the reason why He seeks to keep communicating the vision He has for us in as many ways as possible. If you listen, He will reveal, bit by bit, His plan for you.

I need to mention one thing about God's destiny for us. Although He does have a particular plan for how He wants every individual to serve Him in the world, He allows people to make their own decisions about this matter. And whatever a person chooses to do in service to God and others in this life, God honors that choice and joins her in her efforts. But there is a better way. That way involves a reversal of the above method. Instead of God joining us in our service, it is possible to discern what God desires to do in us and then join *Him*. This is to seek His destiny for us. The advantages to serving God according to His will instead of ours are two-fold: we will find our service more joyful and much less stressful and our service for the Kingdom of God will become much more effective.

4. DREAMS AND VISIONS ENCOURAGE AND COMFORT BELIEVERS

I will give two good examples of how dreams and visions encourage and comfort believers. One vision is Ezekiel's and is recorded in chapter 37 of his book. The context is that Israel had been destroyed by Nebuchadnezzar's

Dreams 85

army and thousands of people were dragged into a sad captivity in Babylonia. Lost and hopeless in a foreign land, many despaired. A majority wondered if God still cared for them or would want to help them. God spoke powerfully to this situation through a beautiful vision He gave to Ezekiel. This vision was a strong message of hope. In the vision, Ezekiel saw a valley full of dry bones, which symbolized the crushed spirit and lost hope of the Hebrew people. The amazing part of the vision is that through the word prophesied, the bones came to life as tendons, muscles, and skin were miraculously formed around them. Then breath came upon the bodies and they came to life, a vast army. This symbolized the promise that God cared for His people and would return them one day to their land. In the vision He spoke softly to His people and committed Himself to loving them and taking care of them.

Another vision that provides encouragement and comfort to a believer is found in Acts 18:9-10. Paul was in Corinth and faced stiff opposition from some local Jewish leaders who sought to imprison him. Paul must have felt some fear and anxiety about staying in that city, because Jesus appeared to him in a vision one night and said: "Do not be afraid, keep on speaking, do not keep silent. For I am with you, and no one is going to attack and harm you because I have many people in this city." This word must have given Paul great relief and encouraged him to remain in a hostile environment to preach the Gospel. In fact, he stayed there a year and a half.

God can still comfort His people today through dreams and visions. One woman from a congregation I served had gone through a time of deep darkness. She suffered through a divorce and then suffered a serious back injury. A botched surgery only made the injury permanent. With the medical care came large bills which she could not pay because of problems applying for disability. She was a nurse and loved her work, but the injury forced her to quit her job. The pain became chronic and disabling. Her life fell apart, and her hope and joy departed.

Depression followed, and suicidal thoughts came soon after that. She just wanted to die. One morning she woke up and looked at the clock. She noticed it was early. As she closed her eyes again, the Lord brought her a vivid and life-like vision. She saw herself walking barefoot on the beach at the ocean. Jesus walked with her and they talked. The woman could feel the wet sand between her toes, hear the waves crashing onto the shore, and smell the enticing odors around her. Jesus talked about His love for her and many other things. She became aware of Jesus' concern for her, His constant presence in her life, and His ability to carry her through the trials she faced. When the vision ended, she had a profound sense of peace and well-being. Jesus had comforted her in a way that was deeply moving and encouraging.

Two months ago, my seventy-four-year-old mother-in-law, Lucy, went into the hospital because of complications from the blood disease she had suffered for many years. At first, we assumed that the doctors would fix matters and get her disease under control. After three weeks, we began to doubt. Lucy did not feel great pain, however, and she was able to talk. On the fourth weekend, Lucy had a good day on Saturday. My wife was not feeling good that day so she stayed home from the hospital. The next morning I woke up early and sat on our living room couch and prayed. I asked the Lord, "Is Lucy going to be all right?" As I listened, I sensed a strong answer in my spirit in the affirmative. I assumed that meant that Lucy would recover and return to her home. To be sure, I then asked, "Will she get back home?" I intuitively sensed a clear "no". I concluded then that Lucy would die soon. She would indeed be more than all right if she died. Death for a Christian is a wonderful, glorious thing.

When my wife woke up, she told me about a dream she had just had. Kay said that she saw her mother in a hospital bed but it was at her house. The room she was in had dozens of bright lights all over the place so that the room was brilliantly lit. Then Lucy stood up and was perfectly healed. She looked happy. The dream confirmed what I had just heard. The bright room represented heaven and the glory of the Lord's presence. In death, she would stand in her heavenly home and be perfectly healed of the physical maladies she suffered. We concurred that both words spoke of Lucy's death. Both of us were strongly comforted because the messages clearly communicated that Lucy was completely fine and in good hands. Within the hour, we received a call from the hospital saying that she had taken a serious turn for the worse. That day Lucy drifted into unconsciousness and was put on a ventilator. Three days later she died. Kay's dream brought us much comfort as we grieved.

God can accomplish many things through dreams. I only addressed four general categories here because most of the Biblical references to dreams, as well as the experiences I know of first-hand, fit into one of these four. God warns, gives information, reveals destinies of both individuals and communities, and comforts and encourages the saints. It is a shame that churches are not taking a more serious look at how God is speaking to His people through dreams.

The problem is that dreams can be misinterpreted badly and many dreams are not from God. It can be difficult to discern between God-given dreams and ones that arise from our own imaginations and fears. But it is possible to learn to distinguish between the two. It may take time, patience and maturity, but it is worth the effort.

One safeguard is to share the dreams that seem significant and from God with mature Christians, and together seek their meanings. Also, it is helpful if you have a refined ability to hear God intuitively. I have learned to discern many dreams that way. If I talk about a possible interpretation of a dream with another person or ponder it myself, my spirit does not rise up to it if it is a wrong interpretation. When it is right, my spirit kicks within me as if shouting, "Yes!" like John kicked in Elizabeth's womb in the presence of Jesus. Also, we must always remember that the proper and fruitful interpretation will usually come only from a revelation from God. I have also become much more discerning of what God is saying in dreams. I have come to identify many common images in dreams that often represent the same thing. Vehicles most often symbolize one's life or ministry. Clear, pure water, often a flowing river, symbolized the Holy Spirit. A birth represents the beginning of something new in one's life more often than it means a literal birth. The same is true of death. It takes a while to learn many of these metaphors, but it is worth the time.

Again, to begin with, share dreams with mature Christians and together prayerfully contemplate the dream. Think metaphorically. Try to get an intuitive sense of certain interpretations to help determine whether they are on track or not. Write down significant dreams soon after you wake up and regularly go over them prayerfully to see if anything new is revealed. Finally, pray that God would speak to you more in dreams, and that you would be able to remember and interpret them properly. If we neglect to look for God's regular communications through dreams, we will miss the fruit of what so many of our fellow believers have benefited from in the Scriptures and who reap great rewards today.

CHAPTER 13:

MIRACLES

Jesus was the great miracle worker. When He lived on earth, He calmed the storm, walked on the sea, healed countless people of sickness and disease, cast out demons with a word and raised men from the dead. Besides wanting to help people because of His love for them, He also seemed to use miracles as a way to get the nominal believer's attention so that he would take notice of Christ, and be more interested in listening to His words about God's kingdom. Miracles are also used by Jesus to deepen the faith of believers.

After turning water into wine at the Cana wedding, Jesus' first miracle, John said that through that supernatural act He revealed His glory, and as a result, "...his disciples put their faith in him" (John 2:11). It was Jesus' supernatural understanding of the woman at the well that so wowed her that she opened up to faith in Jesus. It was also this miracle that motivated her to tell her neighbors and friends about Him. "Many of the Samaritans from that town believed in him because of the woman's testimony, 'He told me everything I ever did'" (John 4:39). This miracle got people's attention and made them interested in hearing Jesus. After they had listened to His words, many more became believers. The people who were converted said, "We no longer believe just because of what you said; now we have heard for ourselves, and we know that this man really is the Savior of the world" (John 4:42). It is evident that Jesus intended for His miraculous knowledge of the woman to be used to draw people to Himself, and then to a saving faith.

A royal official came to Jesus and begged Him to heal his son who was at the point of death. Jesus' response was seemingly out of context, for the man had asked for help, not for faith. Jesus exclaimed, "Unless you people see miraculous signs and wonders... you will never believe" (John 4:48). Though Jesus was disappointed that this was the case, He performed signs and wonders to inspire faith anyway. He understood that people needed something dramatic to get them to think seriously about life with God. After healing the man's son, John writes, "So he and all his household believed" (John 4:53). "So" is the key word here. Faith became possible because the family witnessed the power of God.

In chapter nine of John, a blind man is drawn by Jesus into a living faith because Jesus first healed him physically. In the first half of Luke many of Jesus' miracles astonished and amazed those who witnessed them (Luke 4:36; 5:26; 7:16; 8:25; 8:56). It is interesting to note that Jesus' miracles in the second half of Luke do not just dumbfound people, but also cause them to rejoice and give glory to God (13:7; 17:16; 18:42). The more miraculous signs that Jesus performed, the more people became aware of the fact that the power of God was operative in His ministry. This added credibility to His preaching about the kingdom of God.

In Acts, God frequently performed amazing miracles – usually healing – through the Apostles. It was clear that these were done simply because God loved those who suffered and wanted to help them. But it is also evident that these great acts were performed to add credibility to the Apostle's preaching, and to convince people that God was speaking through them. The result of this was that many people came to faith in Jesus Christ through their preaching and teaching. The miracles were the catalysts for it all.

God speaks through the miracles He performs. He first of all communicates His love in a concrete fashion if the miracle aids some one who is suffering. Secondly, God proves that He is powerful and able to intervene in human affairs for our good. Thirdly, He simply yells, "I exist!" to all who doubt Him or who have no faith.

Concerning the latter, several of my children's teenage friends who are not Christians, and who have never shown that they had any interest in religious matters, have become intrigued with God because our family shares so many God-stories, including miracles and healings. These stories of a Living God have slowly chipped away at their hardened doubt and warmed them to the possibility of God's existence. One of these young people has become a follower of Jesus Christ because of encountering a God who is shown to be alive today through supernatural means. Several who have recently graduated from high school are only open to Christian faith because of the living God they hear about from Kay and me. In fact, several of them have come to me in the last year to talk because they want to know more about Jesus. This never would have happened if it were not for all the incredible ways in which God has moved in our own lives, ways which have greatly enlivened our faith.

The congregation I presently serve has come alive in faith in the past year more than any church of which I have ever been a part. The greatest reason why, I believe, is that there have been four dramatic healings in our congregation in that time, all of which have taken place on a Sunday morning. Each of the persons healed have stood up in front of the congregation and given a testimony of their experience. One man had severe chronic headaches for over a year before he came to the altar for prayer during a service. He was healed and the headaches have been gone for over a year now. Our organist was partially healed of her carpal tunnel on the same day. A chronic numbness in the tips of the fingers on one hand, which she had had for several years, disappeared and has not returned. A woman who had been slowed down because of eight months of regular swelling of the knees walked into church for worship a year ago, stiff and swollen. When the sermon started, the tops of both her feet began to burn for several minutes (heat is common in healings), and she was healed. She has not had a problem for over a year now. The president of our congregation had suffered from chronic back problems, especially in his lower back. One worship service as we were singing "What a Friend We Have in Jesus," he felt warmth in his lower back that lasted for five to ten minutes. There was a healing in his back that has been a great blessing for him.

There is another story that happened this year in our congregation. A woman from the church called me to talk about some matter and happened to mention that she had been struggling from a sleeping disorder. She had undergone tests, but no help had been found yet. Because of the oxygen deprivation she experienced during the night, she suffered from headaches virtually every morning. I prayed for her right then over the phone. She has now gone six months without a headache.

One can imagine the profound impact these encounters have had on those who have experienced them. More important than anything else is the fact they have come to truly and deeply believe that God loves them and cares about their lives. Their faith has been significantly increased. As to the congregation as a whole, many have also experienced a jump in their faith because they have heard these encounters from people they trust. What I have found in so many churchgoers is a very fragile faith that is overlaid with many doubts. They believe the tenets of faith, but can not be sure they are actually true. This lack of faith keeps them from trusting God in their daily lives, and they consequently miss out on the comfort, peace and joy that deep faith in God can produce. I also see a lot if members who have a dry, head-heavy faith that does not excite them or give them any reason to think about God on Monday through Saturday. The testimonies in our church of these healings, however, have stirred up a fresh, vibrant faith in many. It has also had an impact on our teenagers who can no longer mutter, "I see no evidence that there is a God." They are having to take the faith seriously now and are giving it a second look.

I will say it again: through miracles God shouts, "I am here!" in a way that demands all who hear to take notice. For many, it provides incentive to take time to hear more about Jesus and what he has to say. For others, it draws them to saving faith. For all, belief in God is stimulated.

I am not going to share here the many stories of miracles that have taken place in the life of my family and friends, as well as the stories of members of the churches I have served. It would take up too much space, and I have already put thirty-five of the stories together in a book entitled *Miracles and Milestones*. There are so many that I am preparing another book with thirty-five more. Suffice it to say that miracles happen much oftener than the average church layperson imagines. This is because most people who have had a miraculous encounter with God do not share it with others. That may sound odd to you, but it is a strange phenomenon that is extremely prevalent. The two most common reasons people are silent are: 1) they are afraid that others (often including their own pastor) will not believe them, or worse, think that they are crazy, and 2) people worry that communicating a profound spiritual encounter will appear like boasting to some.

The consequence of failing to share these God encounters is that some church attendees have no reason to stop doubting whether there really is a God. These doubts may be stuffed deep in their minds and they may not even be aware of them unless that particular subject comes up. The doubts exist because most people have never experienced a miraculous epiphany of God, nor do they know anyone who has. They believe, but would not stake their lives on it. All the while there are most likely a number of other members of their churches who have had a credible, yet incredible encounter with the Living God. Put another way, these people who have little faith because they have seen no evidence of a Divine Being in human affairs are surrounded by a cloud of witnesses every Sunday morning who could verify loud and clear that God is indeed alive and well.

That is why I compiled stories of members from all the churches I have served into the book *Miracles and Milestones*, and with their permission I am finally making them known to the whole church. My thought on the matter is that a healing or other miracle experienced by one Christian is actually intended for the entire body of Christ to encourage and deepen faith. If they are not shared, the individual believer who has witnessed the miracle may benefit with an encouragement in faith, but others who would also benefit immensely do not. Miracles are to be shared with all to encourage faith and to pass on God's declaration that "I am alive and active in your midst."

I think it's appropriate to close this chapter with a statement that John makes at the end of his Gospel:

> *Jesus did many other miraculous signs in the presence of his disciples which are not recorded in this book. But these are written that you may believe that Jesus is the Christ, the Son of God, and that by believing you may have life in his name.*
> John 20:30-31

CHAPTER 14:

ANGELS

Angels are one of the most dramatic ways in which God communicates with us, and also one of the most uncommon. Personally, I know of only five people who have had an encounter with these heavenly hosts. Each encounter was dramatic. What should be noted, however, is that just because angels are not seen does not mean that they are not present and working to guide and protect us. A good friend of mine and his wife have been awakened many times in the night by knocks, rings and even pokings; they believe these occurrences happen so that they can pray for somebody. They feel strongly that angels are awakening them.

God used angels very often in the events of the Old and New Testament. It has been widely believed that the three men who came to see Abraham and Sarah in order to deliver the incredible news that Sarah would bear a son were angels. Two angels went to Sodom and warned Lot and his family that the city would soon be destroyed (Genesis 19:1-22). An angel spoke to Hagar from heaven to comfort and encourage her when she faced death (Genesis 21:17-18). An angel of the Lord went to the area at Bokim to utter a judgment of God upon the Hebrew people (Judges 2:1-3). Elijah was encouraged by an angel when he despaired (1 Kings 19:1-8).

In the New Testament, angels were key figures in the Gospels and Acts. The angel Gabriel visited both Zechariah and Mary to inform them that God would give them sons who would serve God in special ways (Luke 1:11-20 and 1:26-37). Angels announced the Savior's birth to the shepherds outside of Bethlehem (Luke 2:8-15), and then exhorted them to go see. Angels went to minister to Jesus after he had experienced the temptations in the desert

(Matthew 4:11). Angels were present at the empty tomb to tell the believers what had happened, and to instruct them where to go to see Jesus (Mark 16:5-7). As the disciples and other Christians watched Jesus ascend, two angels appeared and told them that He would return the same way (Acts 1:10-11). The Apostles were supernaturally released from prison by an angel, and then were told to go preach in the temple courts (Acts 5:19-20). An angel told Philip to travel on a certain road where he met an unbeliever and led him to faith in Jesus (Acts 8:26). An angel appeared to the Gentile Cornelius in a dream and told him to go get Peter; through Peter's preaching, God saved Cornelius and his family (Acts 10:3-6). An angel appeared to Paul on a ship that was close to destruction in a storm and proclaimed that everyone on board would be saved (Acts 27:23). John was escorted by angels through his visit to heaven in his revelation on the island of Patmos (Revelation).

Angels are supernatural creatures who exist in order to serve God by both worshipping him (see Revelation 4:6-8, 5:11-14) and being His agents in helping care for human beings. The Scriptures have examples of angels serving a wide variety of functions. They protect humans from bodily harm, as Psalm 91:11-12 states: "…he will command his angels concerning you to guard you in all your ways; they will lift you up in their hands, so that you will not strike your foot against a stone." They also have a part to play in non-believers coming to faith. Hebrews 1:14 says, "Are not all angels ministering spirits sent to serve those who will inherit salvation?" Angels at times convey important information as they did to the shepherds the night of Jesus' birth. They can comfort the desperate, (Elijah, Hagar, Paul in the sea in the storm), commission those called to service (Gideon), proclaim what will happen in the future (Zechariah and Mary), guide Christians in their ministry (Philip), warn those in danger (Lot), and deliver pronouncements of judgment (Judges 2:1-4).

My family's first experience with the reality of angels came when I was thirteen. My two brothers, Craig and Mitch, my sister, Pam, and I all became Christians in the early 70s. One day Mitch, Craig, Mitch's girlfriend Mary, and our cousin Jon were praying together when three angels entered the room and stood silently in one corner. Only Craig and Mary were able to actually see them. They never spoke a word nor moved from the corner.

The four sought God in further prayer, asking Him to disclose what they were supposed to do with their angelic visitors. Jon had a clear impression that they were to send them to minister to Danny, a friend of theirs who did not yet know Christ. After they prayed to this effect, Craig and Mary noticed two angels depart. Then they prayed that the third angel would go and minister to another friend. When they prayed this, the last angel departed.

The following day, these young Christians found Hebrews 1:14. It says that angels are "ministering spirits sent to serve those who will inherit eternal life." The next weekend, their friend Danny committed his life to Jesus Christ through their witness. Here is an example of angels being involved in the work of encouraging people toward a saving faith.

Dorothy, my wife's sister-in-law, has also had an encounter with an angel. When Dorothy heard that her father was in the hospital with a serious medical problem, she rushed up to see him. Her mother, hysterical with fear, was exiting the room as Dorothy entered. Dorothy herself was filled with grave anxiety and fear as she took her first glimpse of her father. As she looked toward the bed, she saw an angel hovering several feet over him for a few moments and she immediately felt an indescribable peace. Over time, Dorothy's father recovered. In this case, the angel protected as well as brought comfort.

Another dramatic angel appearance to someone I know happened to a member of the congregation I presently serve. In the 1940s, Annette had a young daughter who was in the hospital, dying from polio. The young girl was bed-ridden and no longer able to move the muscles in her limbs. There was no hope for her, and Annette was bitter at God for allowing this to happen to her beloved daughter. In desperation, she continued to plead with the Lord that He would work a miracle. One night as Annette lay in bed before sleep, praying again for help, a being of light appeared next to her bed and lit up the room with a bright white glow. The figure spoke and told Annette not to worry because her daughter was going to survive. Her child did survive after a remarkable recovery and has now lived over fifty years since that experience. Annette thinks that it was Jesus, but it most likely was an angel. This encounter brought comfort as well as a declaration about the future.

Although Christians today rarely actually *see* angels, most of us, if not all of us, are ministered to by them on a daily basis. In fact, most Christians believe in guardian angels, that is, that a particular angel is assigned to every individual. There is one Scripture that seems to support this. In chapter twelve of Acts, Peter is arrested and thrown into prison. After miraculously escaping in the night with the help of an angel, Peter goes to the house of John Mark's mother, where people had gathered to pray for Peter. A servant girl named Rhoda came to the door when Peter knocked and became so excited after recognizing his voice that she returned to tell the group that was gathered without letting Peter in. No one believed Rhoda when she shared that Peter was at the door, but after she kept insisting they finally said, "It must be *his* angel." The early believers, at least many of them, apparently thought that each person had a particular angel that ministered to him or her on a regular basis.

It is possible that we have seen an angel before but have not recognized it as one. The Scriptures often show angels as looking like normal humans. Three angels came to visit Abraham and Sarah (Gen 18:1-2), but they had the appearance of three men. Abraham treated them as men and not as spirits, washing their feet and feeding them a meal. When the angel Gabriel appeared to Daniel, he described Gabriel as "one who looked like a man" (Dan. 8:15). The author of Hebrews is convinced that many people fail to acknowledge encounters with angels because they may look like ordinary human beings, and he states, "Do not forget to entertain strangers, for by doing so some people have entertained angels without knowing it" (Hebrews 13:2).

Most of the angel stories I have heard about come from children. I have to admit that the stories I hear sound reliable. One story concerned a little girl who was hit by a bus in Minneapolis and survived. In fact, she had very little harm done to her. When I first heard the story, I simply assumed that the bus must have barely grazed her. That all changed when local media began to call the incident a "miracle." Because of the speed the bus had been going and the manner in which the girl was hit, it was incredible that she had survived, let alone escaped serious injury. The story grew more interesting when the little girl related that she saw a man help her as the accident occurred. The girl was adamant about it. Yet bystanders said that there was nobody there with the girl.

We may need to become as a little child to begin to truly believe in the supernatural provisions of God, including the presence of angels. Our problem is that we have been Westernized, placing an emphasis on what is empirically verifiable and having a deep skepticism when it come to the existence of things that are not a part of our molecular world. Christians often believe in their heads in the supernatural presence of God, angels and such, but deny their reality on a practical level. We need to groom our imaginations and intuition in order to be more open to supernatural encounters with God. Believing in the presence of angels that, although unseen, protect and guide us should give us greater peace and confidence knowing that in the storms and floods of life we are never alone.

CHAPTER 15:

COINCIDENCE

A strange thing about the Old Testament book of Esther is that God is not mentioned once, even though there are ten chapters. This is an odd thing for a written piece that is included in the Holy Scriptures. Yet, as the readers make their way through the story, they hear God speaking loud and clear in the many coincidences that steer the narrative to its dramatic and happy ending. Even before all the events had converged into a united work of the Almighty, Mordecai could see the hand of God. Speaking to his adopted daughter Esther, who had just become the queen of Persia, he concludes, "…who knows but that you have come to royal position for such a time as this?" (Esther 4:14). He meant, "Who knows whether or not God is at work in these circumstances fulfilling his will?"

God's hidden activity in the affairs of the king and kingdom of Persia resulted in the saving of tens of thousands of human lives. He did this all without speaking one word through a prophet, dream, vision, or angel. This movement of the Divine through coincidences of circumstances has traditionally been called "providence" by the church. It is God working out His plans by moving people and events together in a harmony of purpose.

A number of coincidences came together to complete God's work in Esther. Below are the most significant:

> 1. *Esther won more of the king's favor than any other woman* (Esther 2:17-18).

2. *Mordecai happened to be at the king's gate as two guards were plotting the king's assassination. Because Esther was a favored queen, Mordecai was able to reveal the plot to the king through his niece. Because of the seriousness of the circumstance,* Mordecai's name and his service to the king was officially recorded in the Chronicles of that king's reign (Esther 2:19-23).

3. *Mordecai had courage and compassion enough to risk his life* by acting out his plan to save the Jews. If somebody else who had less courage or compassion was in Mordecai's shoes, Esther would not have learned about the plot in time or received the wisdom and encouragement needed to stop it (Esther 4:6-14).

4. *Esther risked her position and life by attempting to stop the* destruction of her people. Another woman with less strength may not have attempted it.

5. *It was imperative that Queen Esther have an audience with the* king in order to start the wheels of Mordecai's plan. When she went to him it was not certain that he would grant her an audience. He did. Most likely, because of how rapidly affairs were going, this was the last chance to start this plan.

6. *Probably the most astonishing coincidence of all, and likely the* key to the success of the plan, was that the evening before the second and final banquet that Esther gave, the king decided to have the book of the record of his reign read to him. Not only that, but the reader just happened to open and read the record of Mordecai's earlier discovery of the plot to kill the king. As a result, Mordecai gained entrance into the king's presence and pleaded with Esther for the king to save the Jews throughout the kingdom.

> 7. *The last significant coincidence was that Haman had built a gallows for Mordecai and when fortunes reversed, it was convenient to use for killing Haman himself. It was almost a confirmation that God was at work.*

In this story, God moved in multiple ways, used a wide variety of people, and then lined up all these circumstances and actors together at exactly the right moments. The amazing thing about this is that God can allow all people to do what they want and at the same time manipulate their actions into a magnificent, well-ordered pattern that fulfills His desires.

I will admit that five years ago I was skeptical about the conclusions reached by some Christians who seemed to read too much into coincidences. Don't get me wrong – I did believed that God would occasionally move circumstances together with the right timing in order to accomplish some grand feat. Outside of that, however, I believed that events and the timing of events were in human hands. God gave up the ability to control human affairs when He gave them free will.

I have changed my mind. I am now one of those fanatics who believe that God is so active in human affairs, and is so concerned about each of us, that virtually all coincidences are providential. The more I have watched for Him in the world around me or in my own personal affairs, the more I have seen awesome, divine coincidences that have guided me in a godly way, helped me accomplish something I would not have been able to do alone, or opened a timely door to care for somebody else. I have also learned that countless coincidences are simply thoughtful acts of a loving God who seeks to bless us and give us gifts.

An illustration of the latter is my peanut story. God moves in the most insignificant circumstances just to tell us that He loves us. My peanut story happened three years ago. I was in the midst of a two-and-a-half year period of chronic exhaustion started by a bladder disease. It was an awful time for me, close to unbearable. We live three miles from the community of Fergus Falls, Minnesota. I had completed my work for the day in town and started for home. As usual, I was extremely weary and just wanted to get to my living room couch to lie down. I was on the street that took me out of town towards home when I had a strange and powerful craving for a chocolate sundae with peanuts. I rarely have food cravings of any kind, and ice cream sundaes are not one of my top desserts.

At that moment, I really wanted a chocolate sundae with peanuts. The problem was that we did not have peanuts at home and I *had* to have peanuts on that sundae, even though I rarely ever used peanuts with ice cream. My mind began to think about the closest place where I could get peanuts. A grocery store was the answer, and there was one only about eight blocks off my present route. That may not sound like a long distance, but I was clinically exhausted. I couldn't face the extra drive, the walk from parking lot to the store and back, and the thought of possibly having to stand in line. That may sound funny, especially to someone who has never experienced exhaustion. But at that moment, even one of the biggest food cravings I had ever experienced could not compete. Needless to say, I would not have my peanuts that day.

Disappointed, and surprised that it was such a big deal to me, I stayed on course. I had only one mile to drive before I left the city limits when I noticed the box for our new alternator sitting on the passenger side floor. It had been installed by my brother-in-law a month before and I had not removed what I assumed was the empty box in all that time. The car I was driving was our second vehicle and usually was not used with multiple riders. That explains how a box could be there for a month.

I had been seeing that box for weeks and every time vowing that I would throw it away that day. It was on this day and at this moment however, that it dawned on me that I was supposed to return the old alternator to the auto parts store for a twenty-dollar refund. I leaned across the seat and down toward the floor to check inside. My brother-in-law had apparently put the old alternator into the box after he had replaced it with the new one.

I was only five blocks away from the auto store where I had bought it and I was set to drive right past it. I also reasoned that because there is light traffic at that store I would be able to park right next to the main door and get waited on immediately. Getting a twenty-dollar refund along with the fact that it was easy to do helped me to decide to stop.

The disappointment of not being able to enjoy a chocolate sundae with peanuts was still bothering me. I was actually feeling sorry for myself. I brought the alternator to the counter and a woman went to the till to obtain my refund. As I stood waiting, I happened to look to my left. There on another counter was a large bowl of salted in-the-shell peanuts, with a sign encouraging customers to help themselves. I was extremely surprised because I had never before seen a business hand out free peanuts, especially in the shell, because of the possible mess they would make. This was a strange and unique thing for that store as well.

What a coincidence! The only time I have ever craved peanuts coincided with the only time in forty-three years I have ever known of a store of any kind that gave out peanuts. It is improbable, to me at least, that these two events could have happened on the same day out of the twelve thousand days of my life. And why, after four weeks of seeing that box in the car, did I remember the refund at that very moment. I was so tired that I would not have come back to take care of it even if I had been only a half-mile past the store. Instead, I remembered it when I was only thirty seconds from the auto place. Add that to the unlikely probabilities which already existed, and we begin to see the footprints of God.

It was not a random or chance experience. It is much simpler than that, and infinitely more wonderful; it happened because God loves Kent Groethe so much that He looks for even little ways to express His deep affection. I have come to learn that He does this with surprising regularity. I love buying small gifts for my wife or giving her a card for no other reason than that my love is so great for her that I cannot keep it under wraps. Coming to understand that God does the same for me has profoundly moved me. I still have to pinch myself to believe that a God so great would love one solitary sinner like me so deeply.

A popular term that many are using to describe coincidences that are God-initiated is *God-incidents*. I will use that term from now on. God speaks through these timely circumstances. First of all, as I noted above, God seeks to communicate His love. God-incidents may be the best means for God to do small acts of kindness similar to a spouse writing notes, giving flowers, or writing a poem for the partner.

The unfortunate element in all of this is that most of these thoughtful acts go unnoticed or unrecognized. As a result, God fails to get the glory and the individual misses His gestures of affection. We instead chalk these affairs up to luck or to coincidence, thus missing God's voice.

Secondly, God-incidents show off God's power as well as His ability to care for His beloved ones. I trust God so much more now simply because I have seen Him coordinate events and people in such amazing ways that I now believe He can do anything.

The most powerful example of this is an incident that happened at a card table at my brother Craig's house. Craig's life and mine, as pertaining to matters of faith, have paralleled each other in the past fifteen years in uncanny ways. The most recent example of this is that in the previous year, we have both been independently awed by how God can move in and through all circumstances for His purposes and our good. It has been the main lesson that God has been teaching both of us recently. His most impressive lesson was when Craig and his wife, Vicky, played bridge with our parents, Paul and Fern. The men teamed up against the women. At one point in the game, Vicky went into the kitchen to do something as the cards were being dealt.

As her cards lay on the table unmixed and while the other three were waiting, Craig picked up her cards and held them at arms length, facing away from him. He told Mom and Dad that he was going to see if he could randomly sort the cards, unseen, into some order. After moving cards into different spots, he laid them back down. When Vicky returned and picked up her cards, she disappointed Craig by saying the thirteen were completely out of order.

Before I proceed, you need to know that Craig was doing this in a silly manner, but because we have learned about how active God is in our lives and able to creatively work in human affairs, he did it believing that many strange things are possible. Later in the game, Vicky left the table again, Craig tried one more time. He told our parents that he was going to try and sort her hand without seeing the cards. He again picked up the hand at arms length facing away from him. He changed the position of about eight cards and then he laid Vicky's hand back down. When she returned she picked up her hand.

"Okay, who sorted my cards?" she asked.
"Why, are they in pretty good order?" my brother questioned.
"They're in perfect order," she responded.
"By suit?"
"Yes."
"In descending order from highest to lowest?"
"Yes."
"Even the suits separated red, black, red, black?"
"Yes."

The cards were completely, perfectly, exactly in order just as we all sort our cards. Before this, God had been teaching us that he can do anything and calling us to trust Him. That day at the card table he put a couple of exclamation marks at the end of this lesson.

Thirdly, God-incidents set up opportunities to help other people or share Christ with them at the perfect time. A great example of this happened last month. A man who is on staff at the church that I serve part-time found out that his nephew, a young man, had been killed. The funeral took place a few days later in a small community two hours north of us. I wanted to attend in order to show my love and support for my friend. However, I could not get out of the office on time that morning because of a committee that had questions demanding my immediate attention. I was forty minutes late in getting started.

I did not listen carefully to Curt when he told me what church the funeral would be held in. Because the town was so tiny, I assumed there could be only one or possibly two churches, and that they would be easy to find in a town so small. I thought I would only have to drive around a little and look for the vehicles congregated together. The town is a few blocks west of the two-lane highway on which I was traveling. When I turned off the highway toward town, I noticed a gas station ahead on the highway with a church beyond it. The church was small and I saw no cars around it. I expected a huge crowd because the funeral was for a young man. I went to the tiny town and it only took a few minutes to go up and down the streets. There was only one other church, but the parking lot was empty.

I stopped the car, confused. Had I gotten the wrong town in my head? I finally realized that most churches in that area were rural congregations and their addresses are given as the nearest town. I had come all that way and it was important to me to at least make it to the lunch afterwards.

I decided to begin a search of the countryside around the town in the slim hope that I might chance upon the church. The one road out of town went either east (back to the highway where I came from), or west. I made up my mind to go west and approached the road where I would turn in that direction. I prayed: "God, am I in the wrong place? I need Your help. You know where that church is. Lead me to it. I am going to turn right (west) at this next intersection. Change my course if it is the wrong way." By then I was at the intersection and ready to turn. As I did, I saw a long train coming near the town. It was getting close to crossing the road that I was about to take out of town. It was going to beat me to the railroad crossing, so I would have to wait. "Is this from You?" I asked the Lord, remembering that I had just prayed for Him to tell to me if going west was the wrong direction. I took it not as a coincidence, but as a communication from God. I turned east. As I was approaching a stop sign at the highway, I saw a hearse traveling south, with the normal line of cars following. It was the procession of the funeral I was looking for. The line of cars was coming from the first church I had seen when I came to town, on the highway behind the gas station. I drove to the church as the last vehicles were leaving with the procession. I was surprised to find a rather large parking lot behind the church on the side I couldn't see when I first came into town. Only two women were in the church when I entered. They informed me that the burial and lunch were in a town seven miles away.

In other words, everyone at that funeral had left the building and nobody was returning. If I had been at that intersection three minutes earlier or later, I would have missed it. If the train had not been there, I would have missed it. If my meeting at the church would have gone five minutes earlier or later, I would have missed it. Coincidence? No. God-incidence.

One morning, I stopped by the middle school in our town to drop a special note into my younger son's locker. I went forty-five minutes before school started so I could do it as a surprise. Only a few kids were at the school when I entered the main doors. I recognized one of the young boys because I had been an interim pastor at his church a few years earlier. I said, "Hi" to him, but I could not remember his name. I went to the school office to get my son's locker number and found only one secretary at work at that hour. It was my friend, Becky. She searched her computer, but was having a difficult time finding the locker number. I went around the counter and stood behind Becky's desk and waited for her. I scanned a counter nearby and saw the Middle School's year book. I picked it up and opened it. The first thing I saw was a picture of the boy from the entry way, out of the hundreds of kids pictured there.

It was only one coincidence, but I clearly discerned that it was a nudge from God. After dropping the note into my son's locker, I spent some time in the hall in fervent prayer for the boy. I interceded for him in every way I could think of, especially that God would protect him and prepare him for any difficulty that may lie ahead.

From the school, I went to the hospital to visit a member of our church, and after seeing her I stopped by the office of my good friend, Ron, the hospital's chaplain. Ron and I got into one of our stimulating theology conversations before I shared with him my double encounter with the boy and feeling that I was called to pray for him. When I finished, Ron told me that he attended the same church as that boy and knew him well. As a matter of fact, Ron added, the previous Sunday that same kid kept crossing his path all morning at Sunday school and church. As he looked back, he concluded that those encounters were both noticeable and odd. He wondered out loud if God was making the boy noticeable for a reason.

We prayed for the boy right there and made a commitment to keep him in our prayers in the up-coming weeks. Within a month, I heard the terrible news that this boy's mother had been in a serious car accident and in critical condition. She lingered in the hospital for days before dying.

Again, was it all coincidence? What are the probabilities of me seeing this boy's picture in the yearbook (out of hundreds of kids) right after seeing him at school entrance (remember that I only picked up the yearbook because the school secretary could not get her computer to work). Add that to the fact that the first person I talked with that morning (in a town of 15,000) was a man who not only knew the boy, but had multiple contacts with him a few days before. Finally, added to all the above, is the fact that the boy Ron and I felt led to pray for was the one kid (of hundreds) at our middle school who had the worst thing happen to him in the next month.

God spoke to us and we faithfully prayed, but I can't help wondering how often God speaks to us, wanting us to pray for someone, and we do not hear Him. Another question I had was: what happened as a result of our prayers? The boy's mother still died - how I wish that our prayers could have changed that! But what else could our prayers have accomplished? We asked God for protection in every way for the boy; for angels to watch over him, for protection from the enemy, etc. Guessing that this call to pray might signify a future crisis for the boy, we prayed that God would prepare him for anything ahead. I do not fully understand what God did with our prayers, but I believe with all my heart that whenever God calls us to pray He does it because He wants to accomplish something by it. My guess is that this boy was strengthened in some extra way because of our prayers or that God sent the right people into his life who would not have been there without the prayers.

A similar incident had to do with my friend Bob, whom I met when I was a pastor at his church six years ago. Kay and I were visiting garage sales one beautiful, summer Saturday morning. We ended up at a sale that was out in the country, on an out-of-the-way road. As I got out of the car, I noticed that Bob's house was nearby. I realized then that we had not seen Bob and his wife, Edie, for about six months.

A couple of hours later Kay and I went grocery shopping and ran into Bob. We had a delightful talk and all the while I was thinking about the coincidence. It was unusual to have neither seen nor thought about him for six months, and then to have some form of contact with him twice in just a few hours. I asked God if He was at work in all this and I discerned in my spirit that He was, so I began to pray right after Bob and I said good-bye. I prayed for as many general needs as I could think of including protection for what might be ahead.

Being sensitive to inner impulses or nudges that come from God (intuition) is an extremely helpful supplement to help confirm whether God is speaking, or what He is saying through other methods of communication. It is my spiritual intuition that helps me discern whether or not a coincidence of two things is a word from Him. If there becomes a coincidence of three or more circumstances, I simply assume that God is speaking and act accordingly.

Later that afternoon I went to the hospital to visit a member of our church. I was not surprised when the elevator door opened and I saw Bob in a hospital bed, dressed in hospital clothes, with Edie at his side. I was not surprised because I am constantly seeing God operate in amazing ways by coordinating multiple events and bringing people together for His purposes.

This has happened with increasing regularity since I have been watching for Him and expecting Him to be active. Bob had just suffered a minor heart attack and was being taken to intensive care for observation. I had the privilege of being able to be there at a scary moment to encourage them and pray with them. I was also able to notify their pastors so they could begin to pray and care for them. Did my prayers minimize Bob's attack? Again, I don't know, but I firmly believe that something was altered for the good.

Joseph, of the Old Testament, understood God-incidences very well by the end of his life. All the major events of his life seemed to be random streaks of bad luck. But in the end, God sewed each of these pieces together into a beautiful tapestry whose pattern made wonderful sense. Joseph expressed it well to his brothers who had caused great evil in his life, "You intended to harm me, but God intended it for good to accomplish what is now being done, the saving of many lives" (Gen. 50:20).

Paul says that Christians "know that in all things God works for the good of those who love him" (Romans 8:28). God works *in all things*. I used to think of this verse as a cliché. Now I believe it literally. God does work in all things in order to help people. The problem is that he has committed himself to respecting human freedom. That means that God will not control human affairs as they are planned and acted out by humans. But once people make decisions and act, He moves in to use whatever is given to Him and without human knowledge, adds other circumstances to it like a recipe and stirs them all together for His purposes.

After bad things happen, we often hear people say, "Well God did it for a purpose." It is vital to make an important distinction here. It is wrong to infer that God wills or causes evil. He does not cause the death of a little girl because He "wants another angel" or because He "needed her more than we do." Nor is He the force giving people diseases or causing accidents. But He does enter into all the unfortunate events caused by human decisions and actions, sin and the unraveling of natural processes to work His purposes. He is like a quilter who gathers all the throw-away materials from people's old and imperfect clothing and sews them together into a well-patterned blanket that serves a new purpose of giving warmth.

God-incidences often happen through repetition. During my years of complete exhaustion, I frequently despaired because I did not know if I could endure much more. During this time I was visiting a congregational member who was also struggling with health issues. In the course of our visit, he said that he had hope because of Paul's words from I Corinthians 10:13, "And God is faithful; he will not let you be tempted beyond what you can bear." I nodded in agreement.

It isn't unusual for a member I visit who is suffering to quote that verse. I probably have heard it quoted an average of once a year in my seventeen years of ministry. But this time, another member I visited the next day quoted the same Scripture. It happened twice more in the following few days. It was striking to me and was obviously a God-incident in which the Lord was giving me a word. I needed to be reminded that God is faithful even in a long period of suffering and that He will not give me more than I can handle.

I want to conclude this chapter with a God-incidence relating to my daughter. It was especially significant because it was the first time that she acknowledged a voice from God that was a personal word for her. Thrilling things happen to one's faith when a person experiences God in a personal way. Cold doctrine and head knowledge of the Christian faith turns into a living relationship with a risen Lord. This is what happened to my Kim.

Kim is a sixteen-year-old girl who struggles with issues typical of girls her age. While talking to several friends on the Internet, she noticed that one friend's address was changed to a Bible passage, Matthew 6:25-34. She looked it up and found it to be a very fitting passage for her. Jesus tells us to "not worry about your life, what you will eat or drink; or your body, what you will wear... And why do you worry about clothes...but seek first his kingdom and his righteousness, and all these things will be given to you as well."

Within a couple days that same message came in two separate forms. I occasionally give cards to Kim with a letter. The notes are always saying general things like, "I love you" or "You are ..." etc. For some reason however, the note I sent this time I wrote in a different vein. I told her not to worry, but to trust God. I did not know that Matthew 6 was stirring in her mind at the time.

The third time she heard about not worrying was when a friend gave Kim a song she wanted her to listen to. The song made the friend think of Kim when she heard it. Kim was awed that it also spoke of not worrying and of trusting God. These three incidents happened only days apart. She was so excited because she believed that God had arranged all of this to happen in order to give her a message appropriate for the time. Kim wrote out the Scripture in order to have it visible, and told her mother about the cool God-incident.

I did not know any of this yet. The same week there was a series of renewal events at a local church which featured a guest speaker for four nights in a row. Kay and I wanted to go every evening and we told the kids that they had to go to at least one. Kim picked her night and the three of us sat together in the back. After the singing the speaker got up and read the Scripture lesson for his message. When he announced that the text was Matthew 6:25-34, I heard two gasps and then laughter next to me. I turned to Kay and Kim and they explained the story. This final event sealed in Kim's mind the incredible reality that the Maker of heaven and earth knew her and wanted to talk to her. It was the start of a deeper thirst for God that has been encouraged the last six months by several other encounters with Him.

We should look for God under every rock and in every bush as we watch our day unfold. Pay attention! God is with us and His desire is to communicate His love, to care for His beloved people, and to draw them into an intimate relationship. As the great 16th century theologian John Calvin wrote, "God so attends to the regulation of individual events, and they all proceed from His set plan, that nothing takes place by chance."[1]

As we become more convinced of how powerful God is, and how capable of moving in all circumstances for His purposes and your good, we will find ourselves less impatient, angry, or frustrated when circumstances go awry or contrary to what we desired. If our car breaks down while we are on the way to someplace important, we won't dare cuss or get angry, because by doing so we would be stating loudly, "God certainly can't do something good here." Instead, we should wait and watch, praying: "All powerful God, you can do all things. I give this situation to you and trust that you will both care for me and work things out. Do what you want."

Notes
[1] John Calvin, *Institutes of the Christian Religion: Volume 1.* (Philadelphia: Westminster, 1960), 203.

CHAPTER 16:

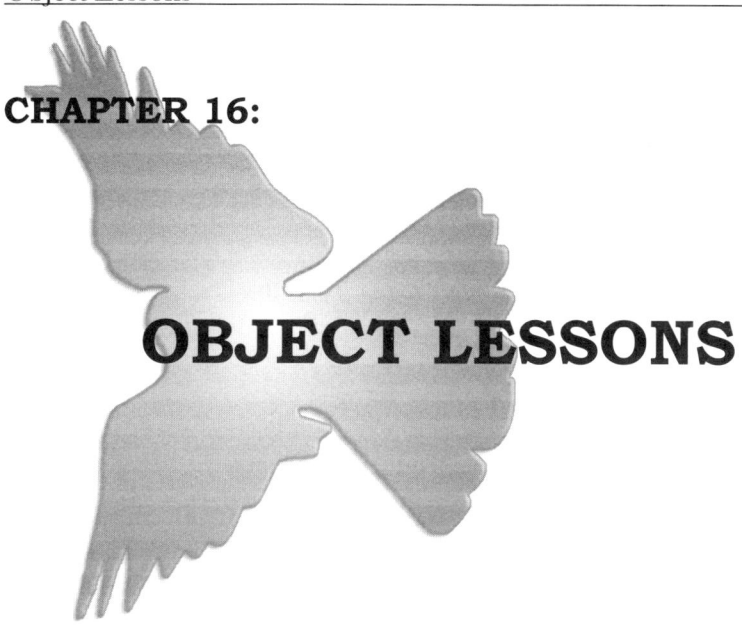

OBJECT LESSONS

God speaks to me personally most often through object lessons. Events that occur around me are frequently timely messages from Him. I have come to believe that God is truly able to coordinate a multiple of happenings in such a manner that they fit together for His purposes. It never ceases to amaze me how He is able to allow people to do as they please and still fit their actions into a larger plan.

So often in my own life events that happen around me are words from God to comfort or guide me. Not everything that happens is an object lesson. Most are not. But when something transpires in the circumstances of daily life that is also a word from the Lord to me, I often intuitively know it.

God often used object lessons to reinforce His message through His prophets. God told Jeremiah to "Go and buy a linen belt and put it around your waist" (Jeremiah 13:1). Next, he was commanded to hide the belt in a hole. Many days later, God instructed Jeremiah to go dig up the belt. By this time it was ruined and completely useless. This was an object lesson whose message was: "In the same way, I will ruin the pride of Judah and the great pride of Jerusalem. These wicked people, who refuse to listen to my words, who follow the stubbornness of their hearts and go after other gods to serve and worship them, will be like this belt – completely useless" (Jeremiah 13:9-10).

On another occasion, the Lord commanded Jeremiah to, "Go down to the potter's house, and there I will give you my message" (Jeremiah 18:2). Jeremiah obeyed and spent some time watching the potter at his wheel before God taught him a lesson with the help of this visual aid. "…'O house of

Israel, can I not do with you as this potter does?' declares the LORD. 'Like clay in the hand of the potter, so are you in my hand'" (Jeremiah 18:6).

God instructed Hosea to marry a prostitute and have children with her: "Go, take to yourself an adulterous wife...because the land is guilty of the vilest adultery in departing from the LORD" (Hosea 1:2). Hosea's wife was unfaithful and had relations with other men. Then the Lord said to Hosea: "Go, show your love to your wife again, though she is loved by another and is an adulteress. Love her as the LORD loves the Israelites, though they turn to other gods..." (Hosea 3:1).

God told Amos to ponder a basket of ripe fruit that lay about. He asked Amos what he saw. "A basket of ripe fruit," Amos answered. Then the Lord used this image to speak about the coming wrath upon the people of Israel. "The time is ripe for my people Israel; I will spare them no longer" (Amos 8:2).

Educators know that a student learns better if visual aids are included in the learning process. The best learning of all is when touching, seeing, and hearing are all components of the lesson. In the church, colors, robes, candles and many other symbols are used to help encourage the mind to understand the things of God. In the same way, the Lord is constantly speaking to us through what we are encountering in our daily routine. The problem is that we are so often oblivious to these voices, and at times even consider them nuisances. In the movie *Bruce Almighty*, the main character (Jim Carey) is driving his car while praying for God to show him some sign that he will guide him through a terrible time in his life. Just then, he passes a sign that reads "Caution Ahead." Within seconds a truck full of road signs cut out in front of him, causing him great irritation. The signs that were readable said: "Caution," "Stop," "Dead End," and the like. The point was that God was giving words of warning to Bruce by the timely appearance of these signs. God's message was for him to stop and change directions. Not only did the character not see this as the voice of God, but was annoyed that it was in his way.

The key to understanding that God is involved in such activity is to believe that God can actually coordinate countless independent events and activities into an overall plan while each individual person involved makes her own choices, unconscious of how God is fitting it into His purposes. I now believe this because I have seen Him work time and again through human and natural events to teach me a message or comfort me when I needed it.

I had just begun my ministry at one church when a man came into my office for a friendly visit. For some reason I began to share with him many of the object lessons that God had placed before me in the previous year.

Before this, I had spoken very little to anyone in the churches I had served about God's object lessons. The following week the man was anxious to share an object lesson with me. He was then suffering from depression and going through a very difficult time in his life. He had earlier talked about his thoughts of taking his life. That week as he was drove his car on a country road, he was overcome with despair. He thought about how his own death would be a relief. He saw a herd of cattle in the field and fantasized them in the road ahead of him; he would drive into the herd to end his misery once and for all. Shortly after these thoughts, he saw a large animal in the middle of the road ahead of him. As he drew closer, he realized that it was a Clydesdale, a horse that I had never seen in that area before. The large animal was blocking the road and the man stopped his vehicle. He went out and approached the horse. The Clydesdale stayed put. The man was able to walk right up to it and pet it. It was such an odd occurrence; happening right after imagining animals in the road, he assumed it was a message from God.

I agreed. I had a strong sense that God was indeed trying to communicate something. The road he was taking that day led to only more sadness and hopelessness. He wanted to die. Instead, a huge beast of burden stopped him in his tracks. Clydesdales immediately bring to mind the Budweiser teams that pull the large hitch wagons seen on television. My wife and I had only recently seen one in a Fourth of July parade in St. Louis. These animals are superb at pulling large loads, including passengers and their gear. I told this man that I believed God was telling him to stop and get acquainted with the presence of Jesus in his life. Jesus, like a Clydesdale, is great at carrying heavy loads and weary people. I believed that Jesus was telling him to throw his heavy load, which he could not manage alone, up into the wagon, then climb in himself and let Jesus bring him through this tough time.

In another parish, I was asked to perform a burial for a forty-year-old man whose funeral took place a week earlier in a city a few hours away. I knew this man's parents because they had vacationed in our small town for years, and were planning to move here when the home they were building on a nearby lake was finished. They often visited our congregation when they were in town.

I met the family and close friends at a country cemetery where the burial was to take place. Most were already present and we waited for only a short time before beginning. I had a longer than usual graveside service because many of these people had not been present at the funeral. I noticed a very gentle dog that mingled with the family. After the service, the dog went to each of the nephews and interacted with them. Since the deceased man had no children, these nephews were very special. They were having a difficult time with his death. It almost looked like the dog knew what he was doing, picking these boys out and comforting them.

As I was leaving the cemetery, I asked a member of our congregation if he had seen how that dog was seemingly caring for the nephews. I made another remark that made it clear that I assumed that the dog belonged to the family. He corrected me and told me that the dog was from one of the neighborhood farms. I heard later that the dog had been lying by the open grave when they first arrived and interacted with them the minute they had arrived. I also found out that during the service the dog sat at the feet of the father of the deceased and laid his head on his shoes.

I was struck by this event. Out of the twenty or thirty people present, the dog found the father and nephews of the one we buried and paid special attention to them. I discerned God's hand in it. The next time that the parents of the deceased man were at our church for worship, I talked to them about this. I shared that I thought this was a word from God. In my life, God has used the image of a dog before to represent Jesus Christ who is "man's (and woman's) best friend," especially in times of need. I told them that Jesus, through His Spirit, was present that day as always. Often in times of sadness we do not see that Spirit and are not as comforted as we could be. I believe that dog was Jesus' way of showing just how His Spirit was present that day, sitting next to the mourners, seeking to comfort them. Jesus is truly man's best friend in difficult times like these. The couple nodded in agreement. They too had taken it as a message of God's presence and comfort. I was quick to add that it was not the deceased's spirit that was inhabiting or moving the dog (as many today are tempted to think), but was simply God using the presence of that dog to give a picture of what He was doing in an invisible way.

A couple at another church I served as interim pastor had a cow that came down with milk fever, a very serious sickness which often led to death. The cow lay down and was unable to get up again. They put her in the yard and nursed her as best they could. On his first trip, the vet said that the cow would not survive if she did not rise to her feet. On his second visit, the vet said that it was hopeless. The cow would die. He encouraged them to put her down quickly. They refused. It was then Holy Week, a good time of year to believe in life overcoming death. Then on Easter morning, as the couple was getting ready for the Easter worship service at church, they looked outside the window and saw that the cow was no longer where they had put her. As they searched for the animal, they discovered her on her feet eating from a pile of hay. What an awesome object lesson for what God can do once death seems to be the only option.

This experience is similar to the timing of Jesus' death as recorded in the Gospels. He was delivered to the authorities and handed over to be crucified during the Passover celebration. This was no coincidence. It was an object lesson that helped the Christian community to understand its significance. The annual Passover was the commemoration of God saving Israel from Egyptian slavery, which started after the tenth plague when all the first-born males – both human and animal – were killed at midnight by the angel of death that crossed the land. The Hebrew people were saved from this plague by killing a lamb and putting its blood over the door post of their houses. In the same way, Jesus shed His blood to cover us from the consequences of our sin and to bring freedom from our enemies of sin, death and the devil. The Gospel writer of John takes special pains to help us make this connection. He seems to put the killing of the lamb for Passover on the day of Jesus' death. Even though this would be historical inaccurate, he conveyed a profound spiritual message. He is the same Gospel writer who emphasized Jesus as the "Lamb of God." In the death of Jesus, he wants us to see that Jesus is the Passover Lamb who frees us from our spiritual enemies.

Another divine object lesson occurred to us a couple of years ago. I remember eagerly looking forward to a Friday night alone with my wife. All three kids were scheduled to stay overnight at friends, and although Kay's good friend was coming to spend the night, we thought she would not arrive at our house before ten o' clock in the evening. That would give us six wonderful hours alone. I can not explain how excited I was about this time together.

When I got home around four o'clock, I found Kay in the barn caring for one of the horses who had just injured her leg. Kay was very concerned and spent about an hour on the phone with the vet and tending the injured leg. I understood the seriousness of the situation and although a little frustrated as to how our evening was beginning, knew that there was still plenty of time left to spend with my wife. She finally came inside and we started to talk about plans for the evening. The phone rang. It was for Kay. It was a friend who had something serious to share. She could not hurry this call, and I soon realized that this friend had experienced a sad event. I was becoming more and more agitated, however, and jealous of these intruders who competed for my time with her. After the long call ended, we again talked about our plans and decided to eat out and go to a movie to begin with. However, before we could leave Kay's friend pulled into the driveway, hours ahead of schedule.

Extremely frustrated, I was surprised to feel anger as well. And to top it off, I experienced strong self-pity. I told Kay that I was going to town alone in a tone that easily betrayed the fact that I was feeling sorry for myself.

Unhappy and blue, I got into the car and headed off, not knowing where I was going. Suddenly, I sensed that the Spirit wanted to teach me something. I became aware that God was speaking through what I had just experienced and that He desperately longed for intimate time with me. He is frustrated when I am too busy for Him and neglect spending longer periods of time alone with Him. He, too, dislikes all the interruptions that keep us from that intimacy. He used this experience between my wife and I to help me better understand God's desires for me.

Since we live in the country, we take our own garbage to the landfill via our old beat-up pickup. This is normally a monthly enterprise, but we usually let the garbage sit for the last few frigid months of Minnesota winters and take one heaping truck load to the dump in the spring. Since winters here are so cold, the garbage freezes and there is no worry about smell or germs. Also, we store our truck in the winters and do not use it.

One particular year, we allowed the garbage to accumulate longer than normal. We stacked the bags neatly along the back wall of our garage. Spring came and the thawing began to unleash the odors of months of waste. I filled the truck and took it to the landfill. I pulled up beside a large metal bin and shut off the truck before unloading. When I had finished I got into the cab to leave, but the truck wouldn't start. The more times I attempted to start the truck, the less energy it had to do so. After waiting a few minutes, energy would return for a stronger first attempt. But it would not start. So I sat, trying again every five or ten minutes.

I had a strong sense that God wanted me to sit quietly. So I did. He taught me two things that afternoon. First of all, as I spent close to half an hour in the truck, I became aware of the activity of the landfill. I had never before stopped to observe what went on there. Whenever I went there I quickly dumped a load and left, unconscious of all that went on. I had assumed that only a couple men worked there. As I watched, I realized that there were numerous employees. One man was making a pile of mulch with a large piece of equipment. Another was working in the demolition area. Several more drove in and out of the landfill with trucks full of branches or leaves and grass from various places in the community. Dump trucks also frequented the landfill from several counties and from numerous towns in the area. There was a whole world of activity I had known nothing about because I was always in a hurry and uninterested in what was going on around me.

I understood what God was communicating. In the course of my everyday life I rushed from one thing to another to complete my list of tasks and duties. Even as a pastor, I often did not pause from my myriad of ministry assignments. God was telling me to stop. He was more active in the affairs of my life and the world than I imagined. And as I stubbornly proceeded with my plans and agendas, I failed to see Him moving all around me. I became convicted that while I was doing my things, God was doing His things with greater effectiveness all around me. God was telling me that in life and ministry, it would be better if I first stopped to see where He was working, and then changed my itinerary to match His. That is what the first disciples were told to do by Jesus before He ascended. While they were anxious to head out and evangelize, they were commanded to wait in Jerusalem for the Holy Spirit. They were told to become aware of God's intentions and strategy.

Secondly, as I sat there at the landfill God began to guide my thinking toward all the emotional garbage I was holding onto in my personal life. I pondered how sensitive I was in many ways and that I continued to hold on to regrets from the past, guilt for the things of which I had already been forgiven, and pain from people who had hurt me with their words or actions some time ago. This was all garbage that I had stockpiled over time and it was beginning to smell. Guilt, regrets and pain were things that, as a Christian, I should have been disposing of on a regular basis. Instead, I had clung to them, even though they served no purpose except cause me agony and waste my time.

Through this experience, I became much more aware of these thieves of a healthy spiritual and emotional life. God was telling me to let them go. They were to be disposed of and cast away. I was totally forgiven for past sins. I need not have regrets for my past actions since God is a redeemer. And I do not have to keep feeling badly about others' opinions of me. The truck did not start because even though all the bags were out of the back of the truck, not all the garbage had been unloaded. I got out of the vehicle one more time and walked over to the bin. I held out an invisible bag of guilt, regrets and worry about what others thought of me and dropped it in with the other garbage.

I have come to hear God's voice on a regular basis through the normal circumstances and events of an average day. He often uses simple object lessons that coincide with what He wants to tell me. I have been guided, consoled and encouraged many times through these simple occurrences.

CHAPTER 17:

ANSWERED AND UNANSWERED PRAYER

For some time, I taught that God spoke to us through answered prayer. The message was that God cares about our problems and is able to accomplish what He wants to help us. I now add that God speaks through unanswered prayer just as much. We often learn more through the prayers that are unanswered because they help us discern God's will. If I pray fervently that God would help make it possible for me to get such and such a job and I do not get it, then I conclude that God has other plans that are worth waiting for.

A common maxim is: "God answers all prayer. Sometimes it is yes and sometimes it is no". Our frustration when God does not answer our prayers reveals more about us than it does about the Almighty. It shows that we may be thinking of God as a sort of Santa Claus whose job it is to help us get what we want. That reveals immaturity. Our wills may want certain things to happen, whether it glorifies God or not. That shows a lack of surrender. We may even become angry when God doesn't do what we ask. That shows that we really don't trust that our Father knows best and is at work for our good.

A story I heard when I was a kid has stuck with me, though I have no idea whether or not it actually happened. During the Korean War an American Platoon became lost. Heavy fog rolled in that evening and compounded matters. The men did not know how to escape their dilemma so they turned to prayer. The request was simple and obvious; "Lord, please lift the fog so that we may find our way home." To their disappointment, the fog remained. Why wouldn't God answer a prayer like that when lives were at stake? Before long the soldiers heard voices they eventually identified as the enemy and they greatly out-numbered the Americans. The fog was the only thing that saved them from being discovered. With the voices as a guide, they began to move away from the sounds until they were safe. That route finally helped bring them back to camp. In this story God answered the spirit of the prayer which was for safety but ignored the method for which the supplicants asked. God edits our prayers to give us what we really need, not what our small minds believe we need.

We often have a poor attitude about prayer. It often resembles a spoiled child expecting to get what he wants. The more mature we become in our faith, the more we comprehend that prayer is, above all else, the most effective way to promote intimacy with Jesus Christ. Out of that intimacy we are slowly transformed into the image of Christ and we surrender our wills to Him. Oswald Chambers says it this way: "Prayer is not altering things externally, but working wonders within our disposition. When we pray, things remain the same but we begin to be different."[1] The more we trust God and surrender ourselves to Him and what He wants for us, the less we care about whether our prayers are answered "yes" or "no". The answer simply helps us to know God's will in that area.

The Apostle Paul had a serious problem that tormented him. He called it a thorn in his flesh. "Three times I pleaded with the Lord to take it away from me. But he said to me, 'My grace is sufficient for you, for my power is made perfect in weakness' " (2 Corinthians 12: 8-9). God did not answer the great Apostle's prayer by taking away his suffering, as he requested. He allowed it to continue. Paul was not upset because he knew that God wanted to work out His purposes through it. Paul did have an idea what God was up to, however, and he claimed that the purpose of the suffering was "to keep me from becoming conceited" (2 Corinthians 12: 7).

Jesus himself made a request to God three times the night before His crucifixion. In the garden of Gethsemane, He cried out to God to save Him from the suffering He knew was ahead: "Father, if you are willing, take this cup from me; yet not my will, but your will be done." Jesus' human nature was revealed in His desire to live, but He wanted God to be glorified more than anything else. God did not answer Jesus' prayer to have the cup of suffering taken away. Instead, through that unanswered prayer, God confirmed His purposes, which included Jesus' suffering and death.

ANSWERED PRAYER

When God answers our prayers, He is speaking to us. Just as a parent's going to great lengths to give their child what they ask for speaks volumes about their love for that child, so also does God enjoy doting on us and giving us the desires of our hearts, at times, in order to say, "I love you."

> *Which of you, if his son asks for bread, will give him a stone? Or if he asks for a fish, will give him a snake? If you, then, though you are evil, know how to give good gifts to your children, how much more will your Father in heaven give good gifts to those who ask him!*
>
> Matthew 7: 9-11

Kay and I do not give our children everything they ask for, however. In fact, a majority of things they ask for we do not oblige, but occasionally we surprise them with something they never dreamed that we would ever get for them. In the same way, most of our simple requests to God for things go unanswered, but once in a while He will provide something special, and in such a way that we know it can only be from Him. It is in those events we see how much God delights in us.

God also says other things through the prayers that He answers. He reminds us that He is there and is thinking of us. He also communicates His power. When He coordinates the answer to prayer in a way only He can, we gain confidence in His ability to do anything for us if He would desire.

I cannot prove this, but it seems to me that God indulges the petty requests of the new Christian much more than He does for the mature believer. I think that this is because He wants to solidify that person's faith in His love and power.

The first prayer request that God answered for me in such a manner that I could not deny that it was from Him alone was when I was about fourteen. I was lying around the house one day listening to the radio. The top fifty or so songs of the week were being played one at a time, from number fifty to number one. As I listened, I was irritated at all the songs with lame or even ungodly lyrics. After a couple of hours when the countdown reached the top ten, I prayed, "God, may the number one song be a Christian song." Right after I prayed it, I realized how stupid the request was. There was no way that the top song that day would mention God. None of the other ones had. I was curious, however, when it came to the number one song as to what God was going to do with my request. I remember how awed I was when the top song did in fact refer to God in a very positive way. Its theme was that we need to be thankful for the things with which God has blessed us. Even after the song ended, I sat dumbfounded, goose bumps revealing my excitement. For a young Christian, an answered prayer like that occasionally helps faith to deepen as God says, "I am here," or, "I am thinking about you."

My oldest son's first answered prayer (that he recognized was obviously from God) happened when he was six. I was throwing baseballs to him and he was batting. We must have played for nearly an hour before I told him that we needed to go. I said that I would throw him three more balls. On the last swing, he hit the ball harder than any of the others, and it traveled considerably farther than the others had. On the way home, he said that he had prayed that God would help him hit that last ball the best. It was an Aha! experience for him because it made him believe even more that God was with him.

I went far from my home town for my first year of college. I was only able to go home to visit once during the year, at Christmas vacation. Tuition, room and board were taken care of, but I was responsible for all day-to-day expenses. I went to school in the fall with money I had earned from working during the summer, but by March I knew that I would not have enough to last through the rest of the school year. When I was down to a little more than $100, I realized that all of it would be gone in a short time. I figured if I was going to run out anyway some time soon, why not give $100 away for Kingdom purposes now. It would be a statement of faith to God that I trusted Him to provide. It was an act of faith in which I was attempting to counter my anxiety with an aggressive act of trusting Him.

My next thought was: what could I do with the $100 so that it would bless somebody? I finally found myself leaning toward giving it to a former pastor who was presently involved in ministry to help unite churches. Sometime later that day, I decided to go jogging. I exited the dorm, and as I did I prayed, "Lord, let me know if you want me to give my money to Harry." With that, I put on my earphones so I could listen to the radio and took off. I was listening to a Christian radio station as I ran. The first song that was played was one that in forty-four years of life I have only heard one other time - when Harry and his wife sang it at a church he was pastoring. I took that as a confirmation from God. A prayer answered in a dramatic fashion has the effect of increasing our faith in God.

Ten years ago, I was blessed to have the luxury of taking a personal three-month sabbatical between calls. I planned to use my time for spiritual refreshment and for some writing. But I also wanted to enjoy an extended vacation. We moved into a small house in Fort Ransom, North Dakota, that my parents owned. During this period, a good friend called and asked if

I wanted to drive to Texas with him. I was very excited at the prospect because I had not spent a lot of time with my friend recently. I was extremely disappointed that I had to turn down the offer because my wife had committed herself to working for three weeks during that period. She was doing this as a favor for her sister, who was director of a daycare center in St. Paul, a place where Kay had worked for three years when we were at the seminary. The daycare was short-staffed for a particular month, and Kay's sister could not find anyone to fill in. Kay was happy to do it, plus the income would come in handy.

I told Kay of my great desire to go to Texas with my friend. I seldom desire something as much as I did that trip, and she could tell. However, if she worked at the daycare, I would have to stay home and take care of our three small kids. Kay called her sister at the daycare and asked if it would be possible to find somebody else. This was an unfair request because Kay's sister had been counting on her for several months, and she was to begin shortly. Karen said that she would not be able to find someone else on such short notice. I was grateful that Kay tried, but surprised at how important this trip was to me. To be honest, I was very unhappy. I felt terribly sorry for myself, so I took my son and went for a long walk, planning to sulk where my wife would not see me.

Kay was taken aback at how much I wanted to go on this trip. After I left, she prayed to God that something would happen that would allow her to stay home and me to go. Within minutes of her amen, her sister called back. She said that after she hung up from the last conversation, she was looking through the papers on her desk and found a note from the custodian at the daycare. The woman wrote that she had an Early Childhood degree and would love to fill in anytime. Karen called her and she was more than happy to work for the several weeks they needed help! How does God do that? He can arrange circumstances that are created by people's own free decisions and fit them into a plan of His own. I was embarrassed that I had sulked and not trusted God to help. Even if He would not have worked it out as He did (unanswered prayer), I should have concluded that if He was okay with things as they were, I should be too. Why would I want to do anything in which God was not opening a door?

God speaks through answered prayer. He tells us He is there working for us, communicating His great affection and seeking to increase our faith. Now let's look at what God says to us through unanswered prayer.

UNANSWERED PRAYER

Unanswered prayer often leads to a misunderstanding of God. If He does not do what we ask, especially if it is a noble request (e.g. heal my daughter of cancer), we sometimes conclude one of several things:

1. *There is no God at all.*

2. *If there is a God, He is incapable of intervening in human affairs.*

3. *He must not care as much for humans as is believed.*

4. *He must not love me.*

5. *I have done something wrong and am unworthy of His concern.*

I think that in some situations, it is possible that our prayers are hindered by unforgiveness or by deliberate and unrepented sin. At times prayers are unanswered because of lack of faith as well:

> ...when [a person] asks, he must believe and not doubt, because he who doubts is like a wave of the sea, blown and tossed by the wind. That man should not think he will receive anything from the Lord.
> James 1: 6-7a

It is my opinion that the majority of prayers that are unanswered are so because God is okay with things as they are and is working out His purposes through what we dislike. We may not understand the whys of His activity, and may even be personally disappointed with it, but we at least know what God's will is or is not. God always knows what is best for us.

When I served one church as interim pastor, there were two men with the same type of serious cancer, and they both had the same odds of survival. One man was in his early twenties and the other was in his early thirties. It was heartbreaking to see them suffer through treatments, thinking that they may not make it. I spent a lot of time with both, mostly in the hospital. I joined hundreds of people praying for these two men. We were praying for healing and that they would survive. As I continued to visit them, I became aware of a clear sense that the younger man would not survive and the older man would. I shared this with the other pastor on staff and she said she intuitively felt the same.

I continued to pray fervently for both men, especially asking that if I did sense something from God about the younger that was true, that He would allow him to live anyway. The younger man died, much to the grief of everyone who knew him. He was a brilliant person who had such a bright future. The older man survived and is doing well today six years later.

A prophet went to King Hezekiah and told him, "This is what the LORD says: Put your house in order, because you are going to die; you will not recover" (2 Kings 20: 1). Hezekiah wept before the Lord and prayed that God would change His mind. God did change His mind and sent Isaiah back to the king to tell him that he would live fifteen more years. King David's prayer for his dying infant son, on the other hand, went unanswered. Nathan the prophet declared to him, "…the son born to you will die" (2 Samuel 12:14). David immediately began to pray, pleading with God to change His mind. He fasted for several days and slept on the ground during his vigil. In the end, the baby died. Then David got up, washed and went to the house of the Lord to worship.

In these stories, Hezekiah and David resemble the two men who had cancer. God knew the future of both and had allowed one to die and one to live. It should be noted that both Hezekiah and David believed that God's proclamations about the future were not absolutely determined. They both prayed even though prophets had said, in essence, "This is the way it's going to be".

The younger man with cancer and David both experienced death. After David's prayer went unanswered, he went to worship the Lord. Unanswered prayer for him was God saying, "This is the way it is going to go." Why some prayers for aid are answered and others go unanswered is a question we can never answer.

"…'My thoughts are not your thoughts, neither are your ways my ways,' declares the LORD. 'As the heavens are higher then the earth, so are my ways higher than your ways and my thoughts than your thoughts'" (Isaiah 55: 8-9). Unanswered prayer is nothing more than God saying: "I am not answering because what is happening fits into my over-all plan. You don't understand it now, but you will one day. Just trust me."

One reason why unanswered prayer is so traumatic for us may be because often our goal is to be happy and comfortable, and to have our loved ones experience the same. When this attitude exists, we are in for a lifetime of frustration, anger and unhappiness. God's desire for us is that we die to our ambitions and goals and replace those with the desire, above everything else, to glorify Him, no matter what happens. After Jesus' prayer for God to take the cup of suffering away in the garden, Jesus tells His disciples, "Father, the time has come. Glorify your son, that your Son may glorify you" (John 17: 2). Then He was arrested.

    If glorifying God in our life is our primary objective, then unanswered prayer gives us a better understanding of what path will best glorify Him. Jesus wept and felt deep sorrow when He asked for a way out of the cross, if possible. Minutes later, after Jesus knew that God had said no to His request He got up and made His way to the cross with a new confidence that through that means would God be most glorified. If we face cancer and probable death, we should pray fervently for healing. Of course we want to live long, find happiness and be safe. But if our greatest goal is to glorify God by whatever means He sees fit, we must add to our prayer: "If my recovery brings You the most glory, so be it. If You will be glorified more by my death, so be it."

Notes
[1] Oswald Chambers, *If You Will Ask.* (Grand Rapids:Discovery, 1989).

CHAPTER 18:

OTHERS

God has consistently opted to use others to do His work and accomplish His objectives on earth. The account of Jesus encountering Paul on the road to Damascus (Acts 9: 1-19) is far and away the exception to how God operates. In most cases, God does not act without some kind of vehicle, be it the Scriptures, dreams, angels, circumstances, suffering or others. When God wanted to preach His most powerful message and accomplish His most important work, He chose to appear in the form of a man, Jesus Christ.

God continues to use humans because He can most accurately convey His love through an agent that can love. For most of my life, I have struggled with a terribly low self-image that has often incapacitated me emotionally. It did not significantly improve when I became a Christian. Sad to say, in some ways it got worse. Now I had to perform well enough to impress God, who could see all my faults and weaknesses perfectly. Of course I failed. I became even more sensitive to my own inadequacies as I was conscious of a Divine Being who could see them even better than I could.

I knew Scripture that stated that we are saved by the sheer grace and mercy of God without our works. Jesus died on the cross while we were sinners and totally unworthy. Jesus visited with the sinful women at the well, accepted the woman who had committed adultery, and ate with tax collectors and sinners. He was the one who told the parable of the prodigal son who, although terribly undeserving, was unconditionally embraced by the father. This Jesus did not consider the performance of an individual as criteria for loving, saving, or living with him.

As I said, I believed this on a cognitive level, but in reality I could not comprehend it enough for it to make a difference in my life. I still judged myself based upon my performance and assumed that God did also. I found no inner peace because in the end I could not love myself. If one cannot love himself, it is highly improbable that he will be able to accept God's love for him on any significant level.

Today I do not suffer from a low self-image. I accept and celebrate Christ's perfect and unconditional love for me everyday. I am gratefully aware of how grace saves me, not my own goodness or deeds. How did I get to this point? It was only because I experienced Christ in concrete ways through His presence in other people. The first time was through my friend Mike during my first year of college. He quickly identified that, because of my inability to believe and accept Jesus' love for me, I was almost to the point of despair. He showed me Scripture such as: "Therefore, there is now no condemnation for those who are in Christ Jesus, because through Christ Jesus the law of the Spirit of life set me free from the law of sin and death" (Romans 8:1-2).

In the end, it was not so much Mike's quoting of Scripture that communicated Christ's absolute acceptance of me as an imperfect person. It was his representing Christ and loving me in His place. Because of our intimate friendship, Mike knew my character flaws and moral weaknesses well. Yet, he loved me and accepted me completely. I saw and comprehended the love of Christ Jesus for the first time through Mike. He was ten years older, and loved me like a father as well as a brother. He concretely expressed that love by saying, "I love you, Kent," and by regularly hugging me. He discerned that I did not love myself and consequently doubted anyone else's love for me, including Jesus. Mike deliberately represented the love of Christ to me in his own flesh. This is the love of God incarnate (in the flesh), which alone had the power to convince me of Christ's love for me.

Kay, my wife of twenty years, is the other great example of an individual showing me the love of God in a concrete form. After two decades of an intimate relationship, she knows me better than anyone else ever has, except God. She is privy to all my short comings. She has seen my deep selfish motives in too many situations. She has had to endure my chronic self pity, overbearing opinions and great impatience. She has witnessed my moral failures and my unforgiveness of others. Worst of all, at times she has been the recipient of my hurtful words and actions over the past two decades. The amazing thing is that she has always forgiven my offense immediately. I don't mean this in a general sense, but literally, always and immediately. She has consistently looked past my flaws and chosen instead to see my best qualities. She has loved me consistently, totally and unconditionally. In that love, I have encountered the Lord Jesus. By receiving this kind of generous mercy, I have comprehended God.

I read a profound cartoon some years ago. In it, one gentleman sarcastically quipped, "If God really loved the hungry and oppressed in the world, why doesn't He do something about it?" His companion responded, "Don't you think that God is wondering the same about us?" This beautifully illustrates the truth of the reality of God's dealings with the world. He accomplishes His purposes through people. We are commissioned by Him to care for the needs of others. If we fail, people are not helped. Instead of pointing a finger at the Almighty, it is most fitting to point it at ourselves. There is enough food in the world for everyone. It is human greed, selfishness, and lack of compassion that are the obstacles to everyone getting sufficient amounts of it.

God has given us two tasks. One is the Great Commandment: "A new command I give you: Love one another. As I have loved you, so you must love one another" (John 13:34). The second is the Great Commission. Before His ascension, Jesus said to the disciples: "All authority in heaven and on earth has been given to me. Therefore go and make disciples of all nations, baptizing them in the name of the Father and of the Son and of the Holy Spirit, and teaching them to obey everything I have commanded you" (Matthew 28:18-20a). God has given us the responsibility of both caring for people with needs and sharing the Gospel with others that they may come to faith in Jesus Christ.

From the very beginning, God established the human community, providing them with all necessary resources, and then commissioning them to help each other. God did not meet all of Adam's needs directly from heaven. Instead He said, "It is not good for the man to be alone" (even though God was his companion!). "I will make a helper suitable for him" (Genesis 2:18). Adam and Eve were called to be helpers of one another. This is a paradigm of the entire human community from the beginning. God gives us each other and provides the resources, then expects us to help each other in all things.

God chose a family (Abraham and Sarah) to accomplish His goal of being a light to all nations and bringing salvation to the world. He chose Moses to go and be His spokesman to Pharaoh and accomplish His goal of freeing the Hebrews. He chose Saul, David, and Solomon to lead Israel. He chose the foreigner Ruth to be the great-grandmother to King David. He chose prophets to speak His words of judgment and hope to His people. He used Esther to save thousands, Mary to bear God into the world, the twelve Apostles to proclaim the Gospel to the world, Paul to preach the good news to the Gentiles, John to share the vision of Revelation and so on.

Jesus is the head and His Church is the body. From His mind comes God's vision for the world. The hands, feet and voices He uses to accomplish His loving purposes for humanity are ours. If we fail, people will go hungry and remain spiritually lost. If we surrender ourselves to His ambitions of love, His light will shine in the world again and bring life and hope to all. As we touch others with the love with which He touches us, Jesus says, "I care about you."

CHAPTER 19:

FLEECES

The term "fleece" comes from a strategy on Gideon's part in the book of Judges to make sure he had heard God correctly concerning the Midianites. The Lord had previously spoken to him through an angel saying, "Go in the strength you have and save Israel out of Midian's hand" (Judges 6:14). When the time came for the fighting to begin, Gideon doubted that God would use him for such a grand enterprise. He prayed to God: "If you will save Israel by my hand as you have promised – look, I will place a wool fleece on the threshing floor. If there is dew only on the fleece and all the ground is dry, then I will know that you will save Israel by my hand" (Judges 6:36-37). The next day only the fleece of wool was wet. God confirmed His intentions for Gideon. Still doubting the verdict, Gideon asked God to do it again, except this time make the ground wet with dew and the fleece dry. It happened as Gideon requested. God was telling His servant to proceed.

Today, many Christians talk about "laying a fleece before the Lord" when they ask God to confirm His will for them by doing some concrete activity that would be unusual in the natural course of affairs. When my wife and I lived in Jamestown, North Dakota, Kay went to a local grocery store one day to shop. A homeless transient stood outside the entrance with a sign which read, "Will work for food." Kay was uncomfortable with his presence and avoided any eye contact. She had heard warnings about people 'like that'. They courted the sympathy of small town folk and then used any money they received for drugs or alcohol. There was also the chance that the stranger was dangerous.

Yet, as Kay shopped she kept thinking about him. She wondered who he was, where he was going, and how hungry he must be. Her heart was moved. She began to think about what foods might be appropriate for one who was hitchhiking. She began to add those items to her cart. But when she left the store and passed the man, she did not stop.

Kay got to our car, loaded the grocery bags into the empty seats, and seated herself behind the steering wheel. But she did not go anywhere. She was overwhelmed with thoughts of the desperate man. She concluded that the stirrings within her to share her food with him could very well be God's prompting. But she was still not sure. Because of her discomfort with the notion of approaching this stranger, she wanted to be confident that the Lord was prompting the act. If God wanted her to share with this man, she would.

As she sat and prayed, she told God that if an Elton John song was on the radio when she turned it on, she would take that as a definite confirmation that what she was sensing in her heart was from Him or at least, a deed pleasing to Him. Kay turned on the radio. The first sounds were the lyrics from *The Circle of Life*, a song written and sung by Elton John.

Kay wasted no time; she went to the stranger and became acquainted with him. She learned his name and where he was traveling to. Her fears left her. When asked, he said he would be happy to take some food. She asked him what items would be best and then went to the car to get a bag of groceries. She returned to give him the bag, some cash and say farewell. Like Gideon, Kay was pretty sure she knew what God wanted her to do, but because it was something that was terribly awkward and uncomfortable, she wanted to make sure. The only motivation she needed was an assurance that God supported her action.

An example of a fleece in the New Testament is found in the first chapter of Acts. After Judas committed suicide following his betrayal of Jesus, there was one Apostle missing from the original twelve. The remaining Apostles were convinced that Jesus still wanted twelve for special leadership and that another man should be selected to replace Judas. After the Apostles evaluated those who had been with Jesus from the beginning of His ministry, two finalists were chosen. There was an agreement that Barsabbas and Matthias were the top two picks. What was not agreed upon, however, was which of the two would be the best or God's choice. Apparently, each candidate had his own backers. Each group must have been sure that the man they supported was the one God desired. Because of the stalemate, the eleven sought the Lord to hear whom He wanted to be the new Apostle.

The Apostles prayed: "Lord, you know everyone's heart. Show us which of these two you have chosen to take over this apostolic ministry" (Acts 1:24-25). What might surprise us is that the means by which the great Apostles of the Christian faith sought to discover God's will was by casting lots. This is equivalent to picking straws. The lot fell to Matthias. All were then convinced that he was the one God had chosen to replace Judas.

Sometimes we are unable to discern God's voice as we seek His guidance. At times we are confronted with two equally good options – at least equal in our own minds. In some of these instances, when all other means of hearing God's voice fail, it is appropriate to put a fleece before the Lord. It is as if we are saying, "Lord, this is an important decision we am making but we do not know whether A or B would please You most or be better for us."

A number of years ago, a good friend and his wife had a financial need. Kay and I volunteered to loan them the money to be paid back at their leisure. We did not need that money and had no expectations of when we would need or want it again. We saw it as a savings plan that would be a nice surprise for us to receive again down the road.

After three years, I had a strong desire to make the loan a gift. I wondered if that impulse was from the Lord. If not, I wanted to know if our gesture would please Him. All our money is the Lord's, and we want to make sure that God did not have a better plan for it. We sought the Lord in prayer, but after a week we could not discern His answer one way or the other.

Kay and I settled the matter with a fleece. On the Interstate as we headed for their home to spend a couple of days with them, we prayed, "Lord if you desire us to give them this gift, let them bring up the loan in our conversation." This was an odd enough request because I could not remember one time in all those years when anyone had mentioned the loan. That evening while we were together playing cards, my friend brought up the topic of the money we had loaned him. Kay and I immediately told them about our prayer and forgave them the debt.

I am hesitant to encourage people to use fleeces. I personally have done so only rarely. Looking for signs of God's leading can be terribly subjective and can keep one from seeking the Lord's voice in a more intimate manner, like spending long periods of time in His presence, listening. I would certainly not encourage its use for any major decision.

Yet, many people have been led in helpful ways in this manner. If you use a fleece, however, here are a few suggestions:

1.   USE A FLEECE AS A LAST RESORT

Employ a fleece only when other attempts at discerning God's voice fail. Using a fleece does not demand that we spend a lot of time and energy seeking the Lord and sitting in His presence looking for answers. While we often only want a quick answer to an immediate problem, God desires intimacy with us even more than having us doing everything perfectly. God often does not make the right or preferable choices clear to us quickly for the very reason that He wants us to come close to Him and spend time before Him. He loves to spend time with His children and even longs to do so. Making a fleece keeps us from that deeper intimacy with Him. We want an answer *now*! He, on the other hand, simply wants *us*.

When we have important decisions to make, we should seek the Lord in prayer, in Scripture and through the wisdom and discernment of the body of Christ. Do not demand quick answers. Give it time. We may need to spend hours sitting before the Lord, asking for wisdom and seeking a peace from Him either way. Seek the Scriptures to see if they speak to our situation. Ask other Christians to pray for us. Pray with other believers over these matters and ask if they have any discernment from God. Then, when we have sought the Lord through these means over a period of time and have exhausted these avenues with no clear direction from God, a fleece may be in order.

2.   USE A FLEECE FOR AN EITHER/OR QUESTION

Fleeces are best used when we are confronted with two equally valid choices. Gideon wanted to know if he was called by God to lead the army of Israel or not. The eleven Apostles had to choose either Barsabbas or Matthias. For Gideon and for the Apostles, either one of the two options would have been equally acceptable. They only wanted to know which way God wanted matters to go.

3.   USE A FLEECE TO CONFIRM ALREADY EXISTING IMPULSES

Fleeces are probably most helpful when we are headed in one direction, but are surprised by a stirring in our spirit or mind with another prospect that we are fairly sure did not come from us. Gideon neither sought nor desired a political or military career, but was stirred concerning a word about him being Israel's military commander. Kay had passed a number of homeless people before without feeling an inner urge to stop and help until she met that one specific individual. My own mind never thought seriously about turning our loan to our friends into a gift until I sensed a stirring in my spirit.

Fleeces may work best when we are asking God to confirm an intuitive sense that we have that would change our present course. When asking for a confirmation on whether this impulse is from God by means of a fleece, it is important that we ask for God to do something that would have a low probability of happening. Gideon asked for dew to fall only on the wool, then only on the ground. Kay asked for a specific artist's song to be on the radio at an exact moment. Kay and I asked God to allow our friends to bring up the loan in conversation when in the previous fifty or so conversations it had not been mentioned. The more unlikely the request, the more certainty that it is God's leading. The important thing to know is that we should continue our present course until we are convinced that God is asking us to change directions.

The use of fleeces can easily be abused. One temptation is to seek a sign from God just because it would be great to see Him work even when we already have a strong inclination as to what God wants of us. Fleeces are also often used because we do not want to spend time seeking God for His answer. Although I caution against using it frequently or unnecessarily, fleeces can be employed at an appropriate time to discover God's design for some decisions.

CHAPTER 20:

SUFFERING

C.S. Lewis wrote, "God whispers to us in our pleasures, speaks in our conscience, but shouts in our pains: it is His megaphone to rouse a deaf world."[1] He later said that it is not difficult to understand why God allows and even encourages suffering in our lives:

> *I am progressing along the path of life in my ordinary contentedly fallen and godless condition, absorbed in a merry meeting with my friends for the morrow or a bit of work that tickles my vanity today, a holiday or a new book, when suddenly a stab of abdominal pain that threatens serious disease, or a headline in the newspapers that threatens us all with destruction, sends this whole pack of cards tumbling down. At first I am overwhelmed, and all my little happiness looks like broken toys. Then slowly and reluctantly, bit by bit, I try to bring myself into the frame of mind that I should be in at all times. I remind myself that all these toys were never intended to possess my heart, that my true good is in another world and my only real treasure is Christ. And perhaps, by God's grace, I succeed, and for a day or two become a creature consciously dependent on God and drawing its strength from the right sources. But the moment the threat is withdrawn, my whole nature leaps back to the toys.*[2]

The Scriptures can serve as road signs that caution one about the danger that lies ahead if he is heading full-speed toward success or security not founded on God. "Dead End Ahead," "Bridge Out," or "Caution!" are yelled at the individual who is dead set on continuing his life's direction with pride in his own abilities and confidence in his own independence. Most of these warnings go unheeded to one who thinks that he is in control of life's vehicle. Although he did not pay heed to God's word in Scripture, he will no doubt have ears to hear when his life crashes into the inevitable false hopes and lies. As he emerges from his wrecked dreams that have been totaled in the suffering he experiences, he is, all of a sudden, open to a word from God.

Suffering is an essential part of a healthy human life. Without it, people would never become aware of the deceptions that chain them to the lies of independence, self sufficiency, and personal strength. The ever-present reality or the constant threat of suffering is the force that awakens dull humanity to their fragile condition, as well as to their absolute need for and dependence upon God. It is God's megaphone that screams: "You are not able to go it alone! You are desperately in need of me!" In his later years of life Malcolm Muggeridge noted,

> *Contrary to what might be expected, I look back on experiences that at the time seemed especially desolating and painful. I now look back upon them with particular satisfaction. Indeed, I can say with complete truthfulness that everything I have learned in my seventy-five years in this world, everything that has truly enhanced and enlightened my existence has been through affliction and not through happiness whether pursued or attained. In other words, I say this, were it possible to eliminate from our earthly existence by some drug or other medical mumbo-jumbo, the result would not be to make life delectable, but to make it too banal and trivial to endure.[3]*

When Adam and Eve ate the fruit, they made a serious choice to live independently of God. In a real way, the fall of Adam and Eve in the story in Genesis 3 is a record of the first Independence Day for all humanity. We have celebrated it ever since. The irony in this case, however, is that instead of independence bringing freedom, it brings bondage of the darkest sort. Living independently of the Creator brings total separation from Him and spiritual darkness. It is no wonder why God placed a cherubim with a flashing sword in the Garden of Eden to "guard the way to the tree of life" (Genesis 3:24), after Adam and Eve made the decision to go their own way. It was not a curse, but a blessing. Nothing could be worse than living life apart from God, and finding success and obtaining a fruitful and secure life while doing so. Our sin is not the ultimate threat to our salvation because Jesus died to cover it. The ultimate threat is that we will never turn to God in sorrowful repentance because we have succeeded in finding happiness and a Garden-of-Eden-type bliss without Him.

SUFFERING DRAWS PEOPLE TO GOD

Most human suffering is the result of losing something that is valuable: a loved one, our health, a relationship, a valued possession, a job, lost hope, lost expectations, etc. We suffer because this world and everything in it proves incapable of satisfying us permanently, and yet we continue to build up false expectations that they will. When we lose those things upon which we depend for meaning or for happiness, our world is turned upside down. We are also shaken by the reality that nothing in this world can ultimately be trusted to meet our deep and permanent needs, hopes, expectations and longings. We must look elsewhere. In these times, God becomes a very real option. The Lord spoke to Hosea, saying:

> *[Israel] has been unfaithful...She said, 'I will go after my lovers, who give me my food and my water, my wool and my linen, my oil and my drink.' Therefore, I will block her path with thornbushes; I will wall her in so that she cannot find her way. She will chase after her lovers but not catch them; she will look for them but not find them. Then she will say, 'I will go back to my husband as at first, for then I was better off than now.' Therefore I am now going to allure her; I will lead her into the desert and speak tenderly to her.*
> Hosea 2:5-7, 14

God's goal was not to punish Israel, but to lead her back to Himself. Suffering and loss (punishment) was His method. As long as she went after her lovers (idolatry), and thought that things of this world were her life and her ultimate meaning, she was doomed to remain spiritually lost and empty. Notice that God's method of wooing Israel was to make the things she loved and depended upon to be too much for her. When that happened, there was the hope that she would return again to the Lord. Suffering the loss of the things we love and depend upon is sometimes the only way that we will look for God because we are desperate.

Many people with whom I come into contact on a regular basis who do not know Christ are cold to the Gospel because they have a sense of meaning and fulfillment because of a relationship with another person, their health is good, they are succeeding professionally or they are achieving their main personal goals. I know that they will not be responsive to God until their most valuable possessions, ambitions or relationships fail them. It is usually a matter of time, although it may be years, before they either lose the things they love or finally conclude that they cannot be fully satisfied by them. When this suffering occurs, I am amazed at how readily they open up to God.

SUFFERING "KILLS" THE SAINTS

God's desire for those who are His followers is that they die to themselves so that Jesus Christ can use them as surrendered vessels for His work. "Whoever finds his life will lose it, and whoever loses his life for my sake will find it" (Matthew 10:39). Even more than God wants us to live our best, He wants to "kill" our desires of the flesh so that He can use our emptied lives as a springboard for the Spirit of Jesus to operate again in the world through us.

The Acts of the Apostles relates none of the acts of the Apostles at all. The awesome deeds done for the Kingdom were done not by men, but by the power of the Holy Spirit. The book would more aptly be entitled, "The Acts of the Risen Lord Jesus through His Spirit at work in the Apostles." Jesus did not want His followers to 'do their best' in proclaiming the Gospel. He wanted them to surrender their lives to His Spirit so He could again walk the earth and do what He did when He was here in body. That is why, before He ascended, He commanded the disciples: "Do not leave Jerusalem, but wait for the gift my Father promised, which you have heard me speak about. For John baptized with water, but in a few days you will be baptized with the Holy Spirit" (Acts 1:4-5). Jesus did not want the disciples to do anything for Him in their own strength because He knew they would fail. Instead, He told them, "...you will receive power when the Holy Spirit comes on you; and you will be my witnesses..." (Acts 1:8).

The Apostle Paul was so successful at doing Kingdom work because he died to himself and allowed Jesus' Spirit to lead his ministry. He claims: "...I died to the law so that I might live for God. I have been crucified with Christ and I no longer live, but Christ lives in me" (Galatians 2:19-20).

It is very interesting to take a close look at the end of Paul's ministry as recorded at the end of Acts. His arrest in Jerusalem and ensuing trials parallel so closely that of Jesus' life and death. Jesus prophesied that He would be arrested in Jerusalem. Agabus prophesied that, "the Jews in Jerusalem will bind [Paul] and will hand him over to the Gentiles" (Acts 21:10-11).

Like Jesus, Paul was arrested. A crowd shouted "Away with him!" (Acts 21:36). Sound familiar? Paul, like Jesus, was taken before the Roman rulers, who would judge the accusations of the Jews against him. They were both executed by Roman authorities. This is not a coincidence. Paul's life looked like Jesus' life, because in a literal way it was. Paul emptied himself so completely of his own desires and ambitions that Jesus' Spirit within him began to dictate the direction of his life.

Paul said: "Examine yourselves to see whether you are in the faith; test yourselves. Do you not realize that Christ Jesus is in you?" (2 Corinthians. 13:5). The Spirit of Jesus Christ lives within the spirit of each believer, bringing him spiritual life. Throughout his writings, Chinese theologian Watchman Nee calls man's spirit the *inner man* and he calls man's mind, feelings and will the *outer man*. Paul often talks about the latter as the flesh.

Even though the Spirit of Christ lives within a Christian's spirit, her thoughts and feelings may still be controlled by her own ambitions and desires. As long as she lives her life as she see fit, God's Spirit stays locked up within, having little part of the her daily, outer life. God's goal for all Christians is to kill the outer man so that His Spirit can begin to have full reign and use of his will, thoughts and emotions for His purposes. Until we die to ourselves and surrender control of our lives to God's spirit, Jesus will be limited as to what He can accomplish through us.

Nee states that:

> *Anyone who serves God will discover sooner or later that the great hindrance to his work is not others but himself. He will discover that his outward man and his inward man are not in harmony, for both are tending toward opposite directions. He will also sense the inability of his outward man to submit to the Spirit's control, thus rendering him incapable of obeying God's highest commands.*[4]

Nee illustrates the above truth through Jesus' words in John 12, "Except the grain of wheat falling into the ground die, it abides alone; but if it die, it bears much fruit."[5] Nee later continues, "The breaking of the outward man is the basic experience of all who serve God. This must be accomplished before He can use us in an effective way."[6]

In other words, God wants to "kill" our fleshly desires so that He can better operate through us for His purposes. It is a very difficult thing, however, to break the outer person because the Christian is often deceived into falsely thinking that he *already is* completely surrendered to God. Suffering is sometimes the only way in which God can bring us to our knees in recognition of our pride and absolute dependence on Him. When that happens, we become a more pliable and powerful tool in the hands of our Master.

Five years ago, my life was almost perfect. My family was healthy. I was healthy. We had recently purchased a house on ten acres in the country, with pasture and a barn for our horses. It was our dream home, one we could slowly improve and alter to make truly our own. All three of our kids were at enjoyable stages in their lives, and I was enjoying the best ministry of my life. I felt great about the work I was doing at the congregation I was serving and my confidence soared. Then, all of a sudden, everything changed.

I began to have difficulty sleeping, which slowly wore me down physically. I was unable to sleep for more that two hours at a time and spent each night moving between one of two couches and my bed. After months of this, I was exhausted. That exhaustion remained for the next two-and-a-half years.

My doctor could not find anything wrong with me. I went to an allergy specialist, but found no help. I saw a doctor who specialized in sleeping disorders and had a sleep test done. No help. I visited a psychiatrist to check out if this was all mental. He discerned nothing wrong. He gave me medication that should have helped me sleep, but it did no good.

After a year of this, depression followed. Getting out of bed in the morning became excruciatingly difficult. My energy, a characteristic in which I prided myself, completely vanished. I had to force myself to fulfill the responsibilities from which I could not escape. I lost my joy for everything, even the hobbies and leisure activities I used to love most. I became a most unhappy creature.

Losing my joy was unbearable. I *never* felt it, that exhilarating feeling of well-being, and I desperately longed for it. I rarely smiled, except when I faked it, because I had neither desire nor strength to do so.

Another year went by and matters only got worse. I remember one morning I awoke and felt normal with a semblance of joy and a little desire to do something. I had my daughter stay home from school just so I could actually be with her when I enjoyed myself. The next day, it was gone. One day in two years! I had no energy to spend active time with my children.

I quit doing simple chores around the house because I could not image starting them. My wife picked up my responsibilities. Mowing the yard was an impossible task. My days off were miserable. Even my vacations were unpleasant. I would return no more refreshed or rested than when I had left.

My sleep continued to worsen. No doctor was able to figure out what was wrong.

One of the losses I grieved the most was that of my writing. With no energy, my creativity dried up. In those two-and-a-half years, I did not have a creative thought to write. My creativity and my energy were the two characteristics in which I had always prided myself. Now they were gone. After so long without them, I began to assume that they would never return.

I had moved to Fergus Falls, Minnesota, to devote more time and energy to writing Christian materials, something I had dreamed of for many years while I served in interim ministry. Those dreams were now forgotten. I began to wonder why God had put those passions in my heart if He did not want me to follow through on them. Were the gifts and dreams I thought He had put within me merely a cruel joke?

I lost my vision and energy for my ministry. I felt guilty because I was unable to perform all the tasks I needed to. I did the basics of pastoral ministry, but no more. I had to drag myself out of bed Sunday mornings and force myself into the pulpit to preach. My enthusiasm disappeared. I went from aggressively adding new programs and implementing new ideas to passively trying to simply maintain the work that was already in place.

I prayed constantly that God would take away my suffering and heal me. Nothing changed. Dozens of people were praying regularly for me. My health did not improve. After two years, I could not imagine suffering like that for much longer, but I began to wonder if I would feel that horrible the rest of my life.

Then something unexpected began to happen. I became aware of many of my motives in ministry and writing. I was shocked to realize how much of my efforts were motivated by my desire to impress others. My preaching and my writing were pregnant with pride. I also began to discern that most of what I was doing in ministry was administered by my own flesh (will, feelings and mind). I controlled the ministry and held it captive by my own agendas and visions. I was able to impress people with my enthusiasm and creativity in preaching, but few were deeply affected in a genuinely spiritual way. In a word, *I* was doing the ministry, not the Holy Spirit. That is not to say that God's Spirit did not seek to use my efforts. It's just that He was limited to an associate pastor's role and had to work with my vision.

My pride, self righteousness, strong ego, selfish ambitions and need to win the approval of others surfaced when I was no longer able to succeed on my own abilities. I also became frightfully conscious of my profound weaknesses and my dependence upon God and others. I lost my confidence and learned of my desperation for God.

I began to earnestly seek God and cry out for His help. I had no where else to turn. Since I was awake many times during the night, I began to spend wonderful blocks of time with the Lord praying and worshipping. Since I could not accomplish all I wanted to in the congregation I served, I began to pray more, asking God to work instead of me.

Two things happened. First, I began to notice God acting in dozens of ways to encourage me and remind me that He loved me and was there for me. I became overwhelmed with the knowledge of how present He was and how much He cared for me. Secondly, my ministry began to succeed more than it ever had before. It was clear that it was not my doing; now that I was more yielded to God, the Spirit began to move more powerfully. I ended up at the right place at the right time so that I became much more efficient and effective. People were growing in faith more than ever. In a real way, I relinquished the senior pastor position to the Lord and instead was happy to be an associate who simply supported Him and followed His vision.

After two years, I finally saw the work He was accomplishing in me. In a sense, He was purifying me of my old self in order that He could play a larger role in and through me. He was seeking to break my outer man so that He could begin to rule in all areas of my person. It was a desert experience where He was preparing me for service by purifying me of my selfish ambitions, and stirring His Spirit in me into a more active role. When I began to comprehend the work God was doing in me, I prayed that God would not take away my suffering until He had killed my flesh in regard to my ambitions in ministry and writing. He began to succeed. I remember one day as I sat on our couch I pretended to wave a white flag above my head toward heaven and said: "I surrender, Lord. I get it. You want all of me. Have your way in my life. Your will be done."

I genuinely laid down my professional ambitions. I was broken to such an extent that I told God that I did not care if I ever wrote again. I also told Him that I did not care if I was a pastor or not. I only wanted to do what would best glorify Him. I was truly sincere about these desires, but would not have been if I would have succeeded in myself or continued in such deep pride. And to be honest, I no longer had anything to lose. My creativity was long gone, my energy for ministry destroyed. It was easy to surrender my life to Him when I was empty and worn out.

I finally discovered that my sleeping problem was due to a bladder disease. I began to get help, and along with God's intervention, I finally regained my energy, creativity—and best of all—my joy. But I was different. I was a lot smaller and God was much bigger. I had been stripped of my personal ambitions and was finally interested in serving God, not myself.

Now that I did not need to write, doors opened for my work. I did not need to personally succeed in my pastoral ministry because I wanted Christ to succeed more. I had a new peace that ruled my life because I did not have to please anyone but God and I no longer felt responsible for what only the Spirit could accomplish in my ministry. In the two years since regaining my health, my ministry (or more properly, the Spirit's ministry through me) has been powerfully transformed. In those two years, six people have been miraculously healed at the two congregations I have served. More people than ever are growing deep in faith. I pray more and listen more for his leading. Jesus is able to move much more effectively now that I am out of the way. This is not to say that the old man in me (the flesh) seeks to daily rise up and take control of my life and ministry. But I am no longer satisfied with the stress and emptiness of seeking my own glory.

That two-and-a-half-year period was hell for me. I never want to experience that again. I can not imagine enduring it another time. But, I dread the thought of not having gone through it. In fact, if I had a choice to go through that period again, I would want the same exact experience. It is, in many ways, the best thing that has ever happened to me. I have discovered an intimacy with Christ I never dreamed possible. I have discovered the key to successful pastoral ministry: let the Spirit lead and just follow. My character and personality have deepened and matured. I have found a more profound joy and peace. I have acquired compassion. All of this, because I suffered.

God uses suffering that Christians experience to refine and purify them of selfish ambition and pride. He uses it to break and "kill" the saints so that they will be more effective ministers in their daily lives. He enters it to form His people into a body that will follow its Head's directives. He uses it to make us smaller and Christ larger. In suffering, God shouts: "You are nothing without me! You are dependent and fragile creatures. You are proud and too self-confident," etc. In these communications He guides us into becoming what He has desired all along—His servants.

Notes

[1] C.S. Lewis, *The Problem with Pain.* (New York: MacMillan, 1978), 93.
[2] C.S. Lewis, *The Problem with Pain.* (New York: MacMillan, 1978), 106.
[3] Malcom Muggeridge, *20th Century Testimony.* (Nashville: Thomas Nelson, 1978), 22.
[4] Watchman Nee, *The Release of the Spirit.* (Cloverdale, IN: Sure Foundation, 1965), 9.
[5] Watchman Nee, *The Release of the Spirit.* (Cloverdale, IN: Sure Foundation, 1965), 11.
[6] Watchman Nee, *The Release of the Spirit.* (Cloverdale, IN: Sure Foundation, 1965), 19.

CHAPTER 21:

GETTING STARTED

God is speaking to you constantly. He is telling you that He loves you, that He is able to take care of you, and that you can trust Him. He is trying to give you hints that will lead you to the people He wants to touch in some way through you. He wants to personally comfort you when you are troubled or grieving.

Most of His communication to you may be falling on deaf ears because you are not yet able to discern His voice. In this chapter I am suggesting ways to start learning to hear Him better.

1. ACKNOWLEDGE THE LITTLE WAYS IN WHICH GOD IS ALREADY SPEAKING

Not too long ago I was visiting a member of our congregation in her home. She had heard me talk about how God speaks today in various ways and said she so desperately wanted to hear His voice. She claimed that she had heard nothing. After changing the subject, she mentioned how only recently she had read her daily devotional and it was a timely word for her for the difficulties of that specific day. She acknowledged that it was not uncommon for the devotional for the day to match perfectly what she needed to hear. She knew that God had made that possible. I brought it to her attention that while saying that she does not hear God, she admitted in the next breath that God did speak to her in these cases through coincidence. It was He who orchestrated the right devotional for the appropriate day in order to encourage her. The woman then had to admit that she did hear God's voice.

The first thing that you need to do if you want to hear God speak is to acknowledge where He has already spoken and thank Him for it. You need to break the habit of assuming that when circumstances are strangely favorable to you it is luck or good fortune. Acknowledge that it is God who is the provider of all things good. It is always Him behind circumstances working in your favor. It is He who brings that friend across your path at the right time, has you read the perfect verses in the Bible when you needed to hear them, and who puts you in the right place at the right time so that you can help or encourage others.

Acknowledge God in the beauty of His creation. Listen to Him say, "I am here" by observing His incredible display of awesome power and creativity in the ordered world around you. Acknowledge that the strong urges within you to do the right thing, and the feelings of guilt when you do wrong, are His voice, guiding you along the right path. Thank Him for the gifts and talents He has given you to steer you to the destiny He has planned for you. Read the Bible with a new sense of confidence that it is really He who is speaking to you through those words. Glorify God for His greatest communication of love for you, the life and death of our Lord Jesus Christ. Look back on the role that others have played in your journey to becoming a believer. Acknowledge that God was speaking through them. Remember the prayers that the Lord has answered through the years, and through them reminded you of His presence. Remember also the unanswered prayers that you are now glad were not answered in the way you desired. Hear God's voice in those events saying, "No, I have a better plan for you." The more you acknowledge God in the ways He is easily heard speaking, the more you will hear Him in new and more hidden ways.

2. PRAY THAT GOD WOULD HELP US HEAR HIM SPEAK

Jesus tells you, "Ask and it will be given to you… If you… know how to give good gifts to your children, how much more will your Father in heaven give good gifts to those who ask Him?" (Matthew 7: 7, 11). If you ask God to help you hear His voice better, you must believe that He will do it. You are asking something that He desires just as much as you do.

Pray often for God to open your dull ears to hear Him when He speaks. Invite Him to speak through dreams, through a clearer comprehension of the Scriptures, and through any other ways He would like. Pray that God would give you the ability to know the difference between His voice and the words from your own flesh or from the enemy.

3. READ SCRIPTURE ON A REGULAR BASIS

Paul states that all Scripture is "useful for teaching, rebuking, correcting, and training" (2 Timothy 3: 16). You need to listen carefully to the Written Word so that it can guard over any other words that you hear, whether they are from the Lord or not. Also, being deeply involved with the Scriptures will give you a clear idea of what God's voice sounds like and an understanding of its common themes.

Bible reading needs to be the centerpiece of your Christian life, especially if you are interested in hearing His voice in other ways. If you want to hear God's voice you need to start with listening to His words that are already easily accessible to you in the Bible. He has already said volumes to you within its pages.

4. DEVELOP GREATER INTIMACY WITH GOD

God does not merely desire to speak to you. He wants to have a deep, intimate relationship with you. There is nothing as wonderful as encountering God Himself. One of the reasons He may not be quick to have you know all He desires is because He is seeking, above all, to spend time with you.

The more intimate you are with the Lord, the more you will recognize His voice and be able to distinguish it from the voices of self, culture or Satan. The more intimate you are with God, the greater chance there is that you will heed His voice and obey His words once you do hear them. Hearing His voice should never be more important than getting close to the Speaker of that voice.

Prayer is the doorway to intimacy with God. I do not mean the kind of prayer which is more of a one-sided conversation where you give Him your wish list. I mean prayers of simply spending time in the presence of the Lord in soft worship or just plain silence, enjoying His presence and listening to His voice. It is important for you to set aside time regularly to spend in God's presence. He desires this above anything else. From these special moments of intimacy will come a greater sensitivity to His voice and a deeper desire to follow and obey Him. This will make you much more open to hearing Him speak through many other means.

5. JOURNAL GOD-EXPERIENCES

Consider journaling your encounters with God's voice. Record every single example of Him speaking to you each day. It could be a coincidence, a dream, a thought or a special verse from Scripture. No matter how small it is, write it down. When you do this, you will become more and more aware of how much God is speaking in all areas of your life. When I began, it was difficult to find an example, but after a while, I had too many examples and finally could not keep up in my journal. Then I began to record only the most striking communications from God.

Not only is journaling a good way to get your focus on looking for God's voice, it is a wonderful testimony of God's presence in one person's life. Eventually I want to put all of my stories together and pass them on to my children. They bear witness to an active and loving God who is anxious to be a part of our lives.

6. BE SUSPICIOUS THAT GOD IS SPEAKING AT ALL TIMES

What helped me to begin to hear God better is that I began to truly believe that He was constantly active in my life. I became suspicious of His presence in even the smallest details of an ordinary day. My suspicions proved to be true as I encountered Him even in petty affairs.

One area of life where people most often miss God's voice is in the events that go wrong or those that trouble us. When your car breaks down making you late for an important meeting, you may not suspect that that God is speaking at that time, but He is. You will miss Him if you let curses, anger, or frustrations drown out His voice. Everything changes when you calmly accept all unpleasant circumstances with the confidence that God's purposes can be accomplished through them, and realize that He may be speaking to you to redirect you for His glory.

7. ASK GOD QUESTIONS

Ask God questions, expecting Him to answer. Ask Him if something that you want to do would be the best thing for you. Ask Him before serving Him in any way if what you are about to do would please Him, or if there is something else He would like you to do instead.

I even ask God if certain actions on the behalf of others are appropriate at the time. I never used to do this because I assumed that it was good for me to help somebody at any time. I have discovered that God always has better timing than I do and often encourages me to not do something good for somebody at a particular time. When he does give me the green light, it is always a much more effective contact.

Ask God His opinions and desires about the decisions you need to make. Do not assume that He is uninterested. What I have found to be helpful is to write down on a piece of paper a number of important questions

I have regarding what I should do. "Should I say yes to serving on the church board?" "Who do You want me to minister to most?" "Should we purchase the particular car we just looked at?" "How can I best show my love for my daughter?" I either put the list in a spot where I see it regularly, or carry it in my pants pocket. When I have a few minutes, I pull it out and pick one of the questions. I ask it again to God and sit in silence listening. I do not always get a sense either way in one attempt, but I keep asking the questions at different times until I feel confident that I have an answer. Sometimes God gives me the answer through what happens in my circumstances.

8. FIND MATURE CHRISTIAN SUPPORT

It is essential that you have at least one Christian friend who is mature in the faith and with whom you can regularly share your experiences of hearing God. It is important that you receive guidance and encouragement in your endeavor. You also need to rely upon a trustworthy person who can tell you if we are getting flakey in your pursuit and if your motives become unhealthy.

9. BE WILLING TO RISK EMBARRASSMENT

One of the only ways you will be able to practice responding to God's voice to help others in specific ways is to simply do what you hear. Risk embarrassment if that is all the harm that will occur. It was terribly difficult for me, at first, to go to individuals and tell them information or encouragement that I was sure God wanted me to pass along. I was worried that I might be wrong and it would be an awkward situation. But it was only as I risked embarrassment that I became more aware of God leading me in ministry.

A friend of mine who has been practicing hearing God recently felt an impression to stop at a certain convenience store. He acted upon the feeling and went into the store. As he browsed through the short aisles praying for further guidance, he sensed that God was asking him to go up the cashier and share simply, "God loves you." If you are like my friend and I, that would be one of the worst things to be called to do. It is not that we are embarrassed about the Gospel, but we are nervous about turning people off to Christ because of a tactless or cheesy witness. My friend dreaded saying such an oft-used cliché to a stranger. He also did not want to be embarrassed. He finally worked up enough boldness and did it. There was no noticeable effect either way to the cashier. Did he think my friend was weird or obnoxious? Maybe. Is that encounter going to do anything positive for the stranger? I have no idea. Was it God? We can't be sure unless at some point we learn that my friend's actions produced some fruit.

My friend honored God by risking embarrassment in order to obey what he thought was the Lord's voice. I would not be surprised if God did this merely to test him to see if he would obey a prompting. Perhaps this was a sort of training mission that served as practice. I admit that something very similar happened to me when I first began acting on intuitive promptings that were harmless if acted upon. In my incident, I risked great embarrassment as well. I did not learn one way or the other whether my talking to these two individuals bore any fruit. I now think that it was a test by God to see if I really wanted to hear and act upon His words. I have to say that that was one of the only times that it was not clear that God had me visit or speak to somebody for a purpose that I quickly understood.

Risk embarrassment when that is the only harm that will be done. It will be necessary if you want to make it a habit of following God's promptings in order to bless others. You no doubt will be right about certain promptings (that they are from God) and probably wrong about others. But, as you learn to distinguish His thoughts and feelings from yours, you will be increasingly more accurate. What will make you want to keep trying is that when God does lead you to the right person at the right time with the right message, it is the most awesome experience you can have. The person usually is overwhelmed that God cared enough to send a messenger to her personally. And the fruit is usually astonishing. My service to God becomes very efficient and effective when I follow God's prompting instead of my own plans only.

Just because God puts a person on your heart in some way, it does not necessarily mean that you are supposed to visit that person or even say a word to him. Many times, maybe most of the time, God communicates a particular person to you because He simply wants you to pray for her. That is the first thing you should always do: pray for a person that whom God's voice or action has put on your heart. Then you should ask God for direction; ask Him whether you should visit this person immediately, later or never.

10. SHARE YOUR GOD-STORIES WITH OTHERS

When God moves in awesome ways, you should be ready to relate these stories to others at appropriate times and places. Christians grow in faith when genuine stories of God's providence, presence and power are related. You glorify Him when you declare His wonderful deeds on behalf of humanity.

> *Great is the Lord and most worthy of praise; his greatness no one can fathom. One generation will commend your works to another; they will tell of*

> *your mighty acts. They will speak of the glorious splendor of your majesty, and I will meditate on your wonderful works. They will tell of the power of your awesome works, and I will proclaim your great deeds.*
>
> Psalm 145: 3-6

A woman from our congregation has had severe sleep apnea for years. One of the most trying parts of it was that nearly every morning she woke up with a throbbing headache, which started her day off in a bad way. A few months ago she called to discuss church matters and she revealed this health problem to me for the first time. After finishing our conversation, I prayed for her. I prayed for God's help with the sleep problem. Sandy felt the presence and peace of God in a profound and physical way as we prayed. The following morning she had no headache. The next morning was the same. It has now been six months since she has had a headache. God spoke in a marvelous way to Sandy through answered prayer, a sense of His presence (intuition), another person and a miracle. She heard God say, "I love you, Sandy. I will take care of you."

I asked Sandy if she would share her experience with the congregation. She agreed, and at a Wednesday evening worship service she shared this event with everyone present. Hearing a God-story boosted the faith of the saints and led to a greater trust in God. Sandy was the fifth person in the past fourteen months who stood before the congregation and shared God's mighty acts.

You need to be careful not to share your experiences with the motive of boasting about how spiritual you are or how much more God works in your life than He does in the lives of others. You need to share in humility or not at all. I have found a perfect audience for my God stories: my teen-age children. When anything great or small happens that I acknowledge as God's voice and movement in my life, I share it with my kids. Over the past five years they have come to believe more strongly in a real and active God.

11. DIE TO SELF

Your own self is the greatest obstacle to intimacy with God and hearing His voice. The most important, yet most difficult, activity to perform in order to change that is to die to self. The problem is to first become aware of how large you are, and along with that, how overshadowing are your ambitions and desires. Pray that God would reveal your self-centeredness. Watchman Nee says:

> *Enlightenment exposes the true condition. Immediately it dawns upon you that you are ten thousand times worse than any of your preconceived notions of yourself. Right then your pride, your self, your flesh wither away and die with no hope of survival...Once the uncleanness is really exposed, it cannot remain. Therefore light both reveals and slays...God always shows us how hateful and polluted we are, and our immediate response is: "Alas! What a wretch I am—so unclean, so despicable!" For God to reveal our true self is to fall down as dead. Once a proud person has been truly enlightened, he cannot so much as make an attempt to be proud anymore. The effect of that enlightenment will have its mark upon him all his days... God's subsequent working, as soon as light comes upon us we should immediately prostrate ourselves under His light and tell the Lord: "Lord, I accept Thy sentence. I agree with Thy judgment," This will prepare for more light. In that hour of unveiling, even noble deeds—performed in His name and in love to Him—will somehow lose their luster. In every highest purpose you will detect the meanest inclination what you considered as wholly for God now appears to be riddled with self. Alas! Self seems to permeate every vestige of your being, robbing God of glory.[1]*

Pride, feelings of self-sufficiency and an attitude of independence will keep you from hearing God's voice to guide or instruct. The stronger you are (in your mind), the less you will hear God and the less He will have anything to do with your decisions, plans or ambitions. Humility is the key to hearing God, and it is impossible to have humility when you are full of yourself. You need to be broken. It was only after two-and-a-half years of deep suffering that I was broken and began to learn humility. I attribute my increase in the ability to hear God to that event. Pray that God would reveal your pride without having to pry it away through suffering.

12. BE ON GUARD FOR UNREPENTED SIN AND UNFORGIVENESS

Watch out for unrepentant sin and for unforgiveness in your life. These two monsters can numb your ability to hear God's voice, as well as kill genuine intimacy with God. Deal with these as fast as you can.

There may be sin that you allow to continue in a particular area of your life. This could be viewing pornography, mistreating your spouse or children, drunkenness, etc. I am not addressing here sin in general, sin which is ongoing and chronic. I mean any sin of which you are not repentant and you allow to continue in your life without addressing it. A spirit of repentance and humility before God can open wide avenues of communication from God.

Unforgiveness is a sin as well, but worth special attention. It has the effect of quenching your spiritual life as well as your ability to hear God. No matter what somebody has done to you, you need to forgive and be released from the destructive captivity to unforgiveness. It may not be easy. It may take the power of the Spirit to accomplish it. But you must head in that direction to begin to remove one of the greatest obstacles to hearing God.

I want to conclude this book with the story of Samuel when he was a boy. The story begins with the phrase, "In those days the word of the Lord was rare; there were not many visions" (1 Samuel 3:1). The young boy Samuel was a helper to Eli, the priest of the Hebrew people. He worked in the temple, assisting the priest with miscellaneous chores.

The Lord spoke to Samuel as he was lying down to sleep. "Samuel," He called out, apparently in an audible voice (senses). Samuel was not familiar with the voice of the Lord and mistook it for the elderly Eli's. He ran into the next room and asked what Eli wanted. Eli told the boy that he had not called him and instructed him to go back to bed. Eli assumed that the boy was dreaming or that his imagination was getting the best of him. This happened a second time and Eli did exactly the same thing.

When it happened a third time, Eli began to realize that the Lord was calling the boy. He then told Samuel that the voice was the Lord's and instructed him to go lie down and wait for it again. When he heard his name called again, he should say, "Speak Lord, for your servant is listening!" (1 Samuel 3:10). Samuel did this and had a marvelous encounter with God. He began to grow in faith and "the Lord was with Samuel as he grew up, and he let none of [God's] words fall to the ground" (1 Samuel 3:19).

One thing you learn from this story is that even though God speaks, it is not a guarantee that you will recognize that it is His voice. In fact, I now realize that God is speaking constantly and if we hear at all it is only a small fraction of what He is saying.

The second thing you learn is that encountering God by hearing Him speak can radically transform your faith into a vibrant, living, exciting relationship with the King of kings and Lord of lords. Samuel was serving in the temple of God all day long. He hung around the most influential religious leaders of his day. He memorized the words and actions to every important ritual. He heard the Scriptures read on countless occasions. He took an active part in the worship services, yet, "Samuel did not yet know the Lord: the word of the LORD had not yet been revealed to him" (1 Samuel 3:7). Samuel knew his religion well, but he knew the Lord very little. This is too often the case today with Christians in most churches. I rarely find a believer who is very excited about his faith if all he has is doctrine about God and rituals. Our young people are bored with the facts and practices that do not deepen their life with God.

The above Scripture I quoted from Samuel seems to imply that Samuel did not know the Lord because God's Word had not yet been revealed to him. In other words, Samuel heard the Scriptures, but the Spirit had not inspired it with a revelation. Hearing God call his name that night was the first revelation Samuel received where he knew God was real. Because he encountered a living God, the end of the story says that Samuel grew in faith.

I have seen so many nominal Christians who had very little real interest in God come alive in faith when they had a personal revelation of the Lord: an overwhelming peace during a troubled time, an unexplainable sense to do something or go somewhere that turned out to be the right place at the right time, a healing or a miracle, or a strong and vivid dream that gave comfort or direction, etc.

Many of my colleagues are adamant that Christianity is not about personal experience. I agree that lifeless, mechanical and dull Christianity is not about experience. But an alive, vibrant faith is all about experience. People do not really comprehend the wonderful promises of Scripture or the truth that God loves them and cares for them until they have experienced God in action. God is constantly present and active in your experiences everyday. If you only begin to take notice, you will bump head-first into Him. It does not have to be grandiose and spectacular, although those experiences are more common than you would think. God woos in subtle but noticeable ways, and may use you in a simple, yet effective manner.

Many of my colleagues worry that I am falsely promising that God is going to communicate visibly to His people. Their fair and pastoral concern is that many people will be disappointed if they expect that they will see God in a special way, and then do not. There is also concern that experience is subjective and untrustworthy. I understand these concerns. I used to be one of them in this opinion. But I can no longer subscribe to those conclusions. God is on the move and He *wants* you to experience Him. Thirdly, Christian leaders are too often unaware of God's voice themselves, so are unable to instruct the layperson. Eli was the most prominent spiritual leader of that time, yet it took him a while to realize that God was speaking. In his first two visits with Eli, Samuel was not helped at all.

One great problem today is that many seminaries emphasize head-knowledge and intellectual understanding of the faith. In my four years of seminary training, I was never told that God can speak today, outside of the written and spoken Word. Even though there is great Biblical support for dreams, healings, miracles, promptings of the Spirit, visions, prophetic utterances, angelic visitations and such, I never heard one word about these in my training to be a pastor. I was not told about God's desire to be intimately connected to us, that He speaks in personal ways or that the Spirit can guide our ministry. As a result of this type of seminary training, laypeople are hard pressed to find anyone who can teach them how to listen and hear God's voice.

We pastors are often like Eli and are unable to assist people in the church identify how and when God is speaking to them. The problem is that if we do not seem to believe in or understand God's personal communications, laypeople will rarely come to us twice, let alone three times. I have been amazed at how common it is for laypeople to tell nobody of their wonderful encounter with God, not even their pastor. In fact, for the first ten years of my ministry, I rarely heard people's God-stories. I did not encourage them nor did I share mine. I was convinced that encouraging experiences was dangerous. I was also convinced that Lutherans did not have stories to tell.

I was shocked when I began to speak openly about my own awesome God encounters and people began to share theirs. I was astounded that there were so many. As I listened, I realized that these profound experiences dramatically changed their faith in a positive way. I often ask these people why they had kept quiet for so long and they shared their fear that they would be thought crazy, even by the pastor. So many of our people are growing in faith most powerfully through God's voice calling them through both supernatural and natural means, and yet the church either says nothing or downplays the encounters.

In my chapter on dreams, I told of a woman in Seattle who was given information through dreams of the location of a missing teenager. The girl had been seriously injured when her car had run off the road and crashed down an embankment and was hidden in the trees and brush. After seven days, she was close to death when the woman found her. What I did not share is that this same woman had received information in dreams about people with needs before, while she was in a different city. When she shared some dreams with her pastor, he told her that dreams were not from God and she should ignore them. Many of our lay people today "run to Eli" to get direction and understanding of their encounters, and are not only met with blank stares, but sometimes even with discouragement from seeing God at all in these events.

In the small congregation I presently serve (60-75 Sunday attendance), there are at least fifteen people who have had profound, supernatural touches from God. Five were supernaturally healed with an accompanying feeling of heat. One 63-year-old felt a profound and supernatural peace in response to prayer just hours after hearing she had six months to live. Dreams gave one woman directions to find her missing diamond and to another woman information that she could not have known that encouraged her to pursue a particular career she thought she was unable to obtain. One woman is a Christian today because, while growing up in a non-Christian home, she had a powerful experience of the presence of God when she felt a marvelous heat throughout her entire body as she listened to a sermon. This experience confirmed to her that God really was alive and cared for her. One woman was overwhelmed by the Spirit of God during prayer at the altar and is now reading the Bible and praying on a regular basis.

Since these stories have come out and have been shared publicly, most of the members have been inspired to a deeper faith and trust in God. The young people are taking a closer look at Christianity. My entire family has been deeply affected by all these God-stories. They have a deeper appreciation of God's love, power and presence in their lives. Several of my children's friends who had little or no faith have been turned on to life with God because they have heard testimonies of people they trust telling them about His amazing love in action.

Finally, you learn from the story of Samuel that it is possible to get better at hearing the voice of God. At first, Samuel was in the dark about the Lord when He first communicated. But at the end of the story we learn that when Samuel grew up he "let none of [God's] words fall to the ground" (1Samuel 3:19). Between Samuel's deafness to God and eventually his not missing a single word from God there were, no doubt, many years of practicing the art of listening to the Divine Voice. He must have messed up a time or two; without question, he must have misunderstood a particular communication or failed to recognize it was God. The same will be in store for us. But we can improve with practice. The rewards of succeeding are immeasurable.

I must conclude by apologizing to all the people I served as pastor for my first ten years of ministry. I resembled Eli on the first two visits from Samuel who neither discerned God working in the boy's life, nor gave him instruction in how to listen to God's voice. This book you have just read is Eli's words of instruction after the third visit. I have finally understood that God is more involved in people's lives than I had thought. I now acknowledge that everybody is receiving communications from the Almighty regularly. And now that I discern it my words to you, the reader, are: go and listen for the Lord to call your name; and when He does, respond: "Speak, Lord, for your servant is listening!"

Notes
[1] Watchman Nee, *The Release of the Spirit.* (Cloverdale, IN: Sure Foundations, 1965), 78-79.

Other Books by Kent Groethe

Miracles and Milestones
Regaining Our Balance

Old Places, New Faces Adult Bible Studies
Genesis
Exodus
Numbers & Deuteronomy

Family Devotionals
Personalities of Faith

Spiritual Growth Resources
A Beginner's Guide to Prayer
Epistles

Sunday School/Confirmation Materials
A Lamp Unto My Feet: A Survey of the Bible
A Lamp Unto My Feet Teacher's Guide
Respect: A Fresh Look at the Ten Commandments
Respect Teacher's Guide
Personalities of Faith Student Book
Personalities of Faith Teacher's Guide

Reorder Information

Bible Alive Ministries
P.O. Box 372
Fergus Falls, MN 56538-0372
Phone: 218-731-0662
E-mail: biblealiveministries@yahoo.com
www.bible-aliveministries.com